Don't Tell Presley!

John Locke

TELEMACHUS PRESS

If you purchased this book without a cover you should be aware that this book is stolen property. It was reported as "unsold and destroyed" to the publisher and neither the author nor the publisher has received any payment for this "stripped book."

This book is a work of fiction. Names, characters, places and incidents are either the product of the author's imagination or are used fictitiously. Any resemblance to actual persons, living or dead, or to actual events or locales is entirely coincidental.

DON'T TELL PRESLEY!
Copyright © 2015 John Locke. All rights reserved, including the right to reproduce this book, or portions thereof, in any form. No part of this text may be reproduced, transmitted, downloaded, decompiled, reverse engineered, or stored in or introduced into any information storage and retrieval system, in any form or by any means, whether electronic or mechanical without the express written permission of the author. The scanning, uploading, and distribution of this book via the Internet or via any other means without the permission of the publisher is illegal and punishable by law. Please purchase only authorized electronic editions, and do not participate in or encourage electronic piracy of copyrighted materials.

The publisher does not have any control over and does not assume any responsibility for author or third-party websites or their content.

Cover Designed by: Telemachus Press, LLC
Copyright © Shutterstock/105195227

Published by: Telemachus Press, LLC
http://www.telemachuspress.com

Visit the author's website:
http://www.donovancreed.com

ISBN 978-1-942899-26-6 (eBook)
ISBN 978-1-942899-27-3 (paperback)

Version 2015.04.29

10 9 8 7 6 5 4 3 2 1

Personal Message from John Locke:

I love writing books! But what I love even more is hearing from readers. If you enjoyed this or any of my other books it would mean the world to me if you'd click the link below so you can be on my notification list. That way you can receive updates, contests, prizes, and savings of up to 67% on eBooks immediately after publication!

Just access this link: http://www.DonovanCreed.com, and I'll personally thank you for trying my books.

Also, if you get a chance, I hope you'll check out Dani's website:

http://www.DaniRipper.wordpress.com

John Locke

New York Times Best Selling Author

8th Member of the Kindle Million Sales Club

(Members include James Patterson, George R.R. Martin, and Lee Child)

John Locke had 4 of the top 10 eBooks on Amazon/Kindle at the same time, including #1 and #2!

...Had 6 of the top 20 books <u>at the same time</u>!

...Had 8 books in the top 43 <u>at the same time</u>!

...Has written 27 books in five years in <u>six separate genres</u>, <u>All best-sellers</u>!

...Has been published throughout the world in numerous languages by the world's most prestigious publishing houses!

...Winner, Second Act Magazine's Story of the Year!

...Named by Time Magazine as one of the "Stars of the DIY-Publishing Era"

Wall Street Journal: "John Locke (is) transforming the 'book' business"

John Locke

New York Times Best Selling Author
#1 Best Selling Author on Amazon Kindle

Donovan Creed Series:
Lethal People
Lethal Experiment
Saving Rachel
Now & Then
Wish List
A Girl Like You
Vegas Moon
The Love You Crave
Maybe
Callie's Last Dance
Because We Can!
This Means War!

Emmett Love Series:
Follow the Stone
Don't Poke the Bear!
Emmett & Gentry
Goodbye, Enorma
Rag Soup

Dani Ripper Series:
Call Me!
Promise You Won't Tell?
Teacher, Teacher
Don't Tell Presley!

Dr. Gideon Box Series:
Bad Doctor
Box
Outside the Box

Other:
Kill Jill
Casting Call

Young Adult:
A Kiss for Luck (Kindle Only)

Non-Fiction:
How I Sold 1 Million eBooks in 5 Months!

*For Ricky Locke, who told me things about
James Quelvin I didn't know;
For Stay Busy, the porter, and all who appreciate true beauty;
For those who found their soul mates at the Journey's End;
For mail boxes, flashlights, and phone calls late at night;
For the lucky ones who lit up the world:
Bless you all!*

Don't Tell Presley!

Chapter 1

SUCH IS HER BEAUTY, Stay Busy the porter stops in his tracks, abandons his broom at Gate 16, and crosses the corridor, seeking nothing more than to be in her presence.

SUCH IS HER BEAUTY, the well-dressed businessman suddenly realizes he's about to miss his flight. He jumps to his feet, quick-walks to the boarding area, hands his ticket to the gate attendant, turns to give her one last look.

SUCH IS HER BEAUTY, the gate attendant's eyes never blink while announcing the final boarding call. He studies her like a pawnshop owner evaluates a flawless diamond before offering twice the going rate—because anything less would be sacrilege.

NOW, SITTING IN THE ROW BEHIND HER, close enough to inhale her scent, Stay Busy hears her on the phone, saying, "I *have* thought about it, Ron. I just...I can't do this anymore." She listens a moment, then says, "Wait. I led *you* on? *Seriously?*" She laughs derisively, then listens some more. "I'm acting *immature*? No shit? Well, *newsflash*, Ron: I'm twenty-two, you're thirty-nine. What did you expect?" More listening, then, "Fine, whatever. It doesn't matter. It's over. I'm not coming." A brief pause; then, "I'm sorry you feel that way, but it's over. Please don't call me again."

She ends the call, tucks her phone in her handbag, watches the gate attendant close the door to the jet way. Sits there a moment, staring at the plane through floor-to-ceiling windows, then gets to her feet; walks away.

Stay Busy's eyes take in the glorious sway of her hips as her impossibly long legs move her further from his world. He sighs, remembering conquests from his youth.

As the gate attendant exits the gate area, Stay Busy watches the plane taxi to the runway, watches it take off. Never having flown before, he wonders what it would be like to soar over the city. He tracks the plane with his eyes as it rises higher and higher against the glorious sunset. Then his expression changes to horror as the plane appears to lose power, pitches, and plummets into a death-spiral. He doesn't see the crash, but hears it, and sees the smoke billowing up from the crash site.

Fourteen minutes later the beautiful young lady's cell phone rings for twelve seconds, then goes to voicemail. Then rings again, and goes unanswered. The beautiful lady's name is Presley, and she wants to answer her phone. Unfortunately, her persistent caller has chosen a bad time, as Presley's bent face-down over the hood of her car, in a mall parking lot, with a knife to her throat, getting savagely raped by a man who promised not to hurt her as long as she remains quiet.

Chapter 2

PRESLEY LIFTS HER HEAD to see if someone—*anyone!*—might come to her aid. It's dusky, but not dark yet, and people are scattered throughout the parking area. If someone would just take the time to look in her direction...

But no.

Having heard news of the plane crash, they're racing to cars with phones to their ears, focused on getting home to loved ones.

By the time Presley's phone rings a third time, her rapist has fled the scene. Again, she can't answer, since the man said not to move a muscle for thirty seconds, or he'll kill her in her sleep. "Maybe not tonight," he said, "but soon." And though he has no idea where she lives, that will change when he goes through her wallet.

Fully aware her ass is on public display, Presley keeps counting till she gets to thirty. That was part of the deal, after all, and she's perfectly willing to push aside her anger, outrage, dignity, and tears if it means surviving the most stressful half-hour of her life. A thirty-minute period during which she (1) ended her long-term affair; (2) avoided death by plane crash at the last possible minute; and (3) pulled off the highway into a mall parking lot to call her husband, only to be raped.

Maybe it's shock, or the suddenness of the assault, or the accumulation of events, but for now Presley feels only one emotion:

Gratitude.

She's grateful she ended the affair. Grateful she didn't board the plane. Grateful her rapist left her alive and unmarked, save for whatever damage he may have done to her private area. Nor did he steal her car, keys, or handbag.

Just her wallet.

Presley takes a deep breath. Using elbows first, then hands, she pushes herself to a standing position...and nearly falls to the pavement when her knees buckle. She catches herself, balances against the side of the car till her shaky legs feel sturdy enough to support her weight.

Astonishingly, the assault took no more than a minute. Sixty seconds for the rape, thirty more to let him get away with it.

Except he's not going to get away with it because she saw his face.

Chapter 3

NOW, STANDING BESIDE HER CAR in a mall parking lot with her jeans and panties around her knees, Presley feels utterly invisible. Were she to say something in her normal speaking voice, five or six people are close enough to hear. How's it possible they never saw the crime? How's it possible they don't see her now, as she pulls up her jeans?

These same shoppers will freak if she decides to report the crime. They'll hear it on the eleven o'clock news and say, "Omigod! I was right there!" or, "Can you believe someone would rape a woman right in the middle of the *parking* lot?"

Yeah, she'd believe it.

Her phone rings again, and this time she answers.

"Hello?"

"Presley?"

"Yes?"

He pauses. "You're alive?"

Before she has time to respond, he says, "Mrs. French, this is Officer Eagen, Nashville Police Department. I'm afraid your husband has been seriously injured in an auto accident. He's being rushed to Hailey Memorial."

"What?"

"Mitchell French is your husband?"

"Y-yes, but—"

"He's been seriously injured. You're aware of the plane crash? He was one of the motorists in the area where the debris hit."

Presley swoons. Her head feels like...like someone put her brains in a blender and pressed liquefy. "This—" she shakes her head. "...Can't be *happening!*" she screams. "Is he...I mean, how bad—"

"I can only tell you Mitchell was alive and semi-responsive when I got to him. He was upset, said you were on the plane, and begged me to call you. I tried, but couldn't get an answer, so we assumed the worst. I turned him over to the paramedics, but saved your number and wanted to try one last time. Normally I'd arrange transportation for you to the hospital, but the city's a madhouse, and we can't spare the personnel. I wish I could say more, *do* more, but I have others to notify. I wish your husband well."

He hangs up.

Chapter 4

HAILEY MEMORIAL LOOKS LIKE a scene from a disaster movie: ambulances, bloody victims, cop cars, traffic jams, news vans, choppers in the air, reporters on the ground; scores of distraught family members ditching cars, running to the emergency room, seeking loved ones...

It takes Presley twenty minutes to get from the nearest parking space to the emergency entrance, and ten more to find her husband's gurney. When she calls his name he attempts to open his eyes.

"*Press?*"

She smiles, kisses his forehead. "You haven't called me that in a long time."

He gets his eyes open long enough to see her, then passes out.

Ten hours later, in a room that's only private because two other patients died, Mitch opens his eyes and tries to speak. But his voice is too raspy.

"Hi baby," Presley says. "Here, drink some water." As he does, she says, "You're gonna be okay, thank God." She pauses. "*We're* gonna be okay. From now on. I promise!"

After some false starts, Mitch finds his voice. "You...weren't on the plane?"

"No."

"Why not?"

She lowers her eyes. "I changed my mind at the last minute."

"Why?"

She shrugs.

He says, "Thank God, right?"

She nods.

Now, speaking clearly, he says, "What about your grandmother?"

"Granny can wait. I'd rather be with you."

He looks her over. "You're dressed awfully fancy for a visit to grandma's house."

Presley says nothing.

Mitch says, "The policeman spoke to Chelsea. She said she'd notify our parents, so that's one less thing you'll have to deal with."

"I called Chelsea *and* your parents from the ER," Presley says, "but you know the drill: they all hate me, and refused to take my call. So I left messages. I assume everyone's coming, but they'll have to drive, since all passenger flights have been canceled till further notice. You want me to call them from *your* phone? Maybe they'll answer."

"I expect my phone is somewhere in the car, or what's left of it." He waits a minute before saying, "Can I ask you something?"

"Of course!"

"Where were you when you found out?"

"About you? Or the plane crash?"

"Me."

"Midland Mall."

"You were *shopping*?"

"No, silly. I got as far as the airport gate before changing my mind. When the plane took off I was in the underground parking lot, getting my car, so I had no idea it crashed. When I got on the Interstate I saw the smoke coming from downtown, so I turned on the radio and heard the report and realized that's the plane I was supposed to be on!"

"So you drove to the *mall*?"

"All I could think about was calling you, but I was scared to do it while driving. Cars were cutting in and out of traffic, flying around a hundred miles an hour, changing lanes."

"So you...what?"

"Pulled off at the next exit and turned into the first entrance."

"Midland Mall?"

She nods. "I was hyperventilating, so I parked the car, got out, started walking to clear my head."

"I'm confused."

"Why *wouldn't* you be? They're pumping all sorts of drugs through your body!" She winks. "I'm jealous."

"It's not the drugs. I'm trying to understand why you didn't answer your phone."

"You mean Officer Eagen? I *did* speak to him."

Mitch frowns. "When?"

"Soon as I got back in the car."

He studies her face. "He called several times."

"I understand that, Mitch. Like I said, I was walking, trying to clear my head. When I got back to the car, I heard the phone ringing, and Officer Eagen told me what happened."

Mitch suddenly grabs the side of his head and winces with pain.

"What's wrong?" Presley says.

"I—*Oh God!*" he gasps.

"Mitch! Are you all right?"

He grits his teeth against the pain.

"Press the button for the nurse!" she says. Then, seeing he can't, she reaches over his convulsing body and presses it several times.

When Mitch opens his eyes, she says, "We almost lost you."

"When?"

"A couple hours ago. You had a seizure."

"That was...*hours* ago?"

Presley nods. Noticing tears welling up in his eyes, she asks, "Are you in pain, honey?"

"I think I'm dying."

"No. You just had a seizure. You're gonna be fine."

He says, "You've been by my side the whole time?"

"Of course. I love you."

"I doubt that. The way you've been acting lately?"

She nods. "I know. That's my fault. I was mixed up for a while. You know, about what was really important to me. But that's behind us. I'm gonna be better. I promise."

Mitch closes his eyes for what seems like a full minute. When he finally opens them he says, "I need to tell you something, Press." He looks around to make sure they're alone, then motions her closer: "I know all about your affair."

Presley starts to say something, but Mitch says, "Please don't deny it. I know pretty much everything: his name, address, where he works…." He sighs. "I've known for months. Kept hoping you'd end it, and we wouldn't have to discuss it, but then I realized you were in love, and I won't lie, it really hurt. But seeing you here, like this?" He shakes his head. "None of that matters. I forgive you. I honestly do. It's all water under the bridge. I want you to remember that about me."

"What are you trying to say?"

"I'm dying, Press."

She starts to say something, but he holds up his hand. "I've done something terrible," he says, "and I need to fix it."

"What are you talking about?"

"I…hired someone."

"What do you mean?"

"To kill you."

Presley's eyes bug out. Then she thinks about it a minute and smiles. "That's crazy, Mitch. First of all, you're gonna be okay. Second, I've never cheated on you, and that's the truth. Whatever you *think* happened, you're mistaken. Third, you're an accountant. I mean, where would *you* find a hit man? And if you did, where would you get the money to *pay* him?" She sighs. "Stop being silly, Mitch. Lie back and go to sleep. Everything's good."

"It's *not* good, Press. This guy's gonna kill you, and I don't know how to stop him. He's been following you around for days."

She shakes her head, shows him a skeptical look. "How's he supposed to kill me?"

"I...have no idea. I didn't ask. I was so upset about the affair. All those months, it was eating me alive. I couldn't think straight. Then I met this guy. It was a fluke, a one-in-a-million. He caught me at the exact wrong time, at the lowest point and...I cashed out my life insurance policy and paid him, and...oh God, Press, I'm so *sorry*."

"You're *scaring* me, Mitch. I know you're on drugs and all, but the way you're looking at me, and the sound of your voice...it almost sounds true."

"I swear to God it's true, Press. But I wish like hell it wasn't." He thinks a minute, then says, "*Fuck!*"

"What?"

"The only way I can contact him is—I mean, I probably can't contact him at *all!* Not from *here!*"

It's starting to hit her. "What are you *saying*, Mitch?"

"I need to get out of here, got to figure a way to contact this guy. If I don't, he'll kill you, sure as shit."

"Mitch, look at me. Tell me you're joking."

"I'm not. Every word I've told you is true." His lips quiver. "Press, you've got to promise me something:

whatever happens, promise you won't go home till I get this worked out. And stay away from your friends and relatives. And *my* relatives! And anyplace you'd normally go. You need to change your routine." He pauses a minute, then says, "*Omigod!*"

"What?"

"The plane! Did it crash or explode?"

Presley's eyes grow wide. "It crashed right after takeoff, but they're not sure if it was pilot error or...wait. Surely you're not saying..."

The look of horror remains on Mitch's face as he asks, "Was Ron the pilot?"

The question catches her off-guard.

"Ron Sallow," he adds. "Your boyfriend."

"He's not my boyfriend. We're workout friends, nothing more."

"Never met in public, outside the gym?"

She sighs. "Yes. But it's not what you think."

"Was he flying the plane tonight?"

Presley can't hold it in any more. She starts crying.

Mitch's features harden. "I'm sorry for your loss, Presley. Guess that makes me the only game in town. No wonder you've been so attentive."

It takes her a minute to compose herself. "I chose you already. It's the reason I never got on the plane."

"Lover's quarrel?"

"Whatever it was, I ended it."

"While we're on the subject, what exactly *was* it, Press?"

"We were close."

"Close?"

"A lot closer than I let on. But...I didn't love him, Mitch. Swear to God."

"That's awfully hard to believe, under the circumstances." He grimaces in pain, then swallows and says, "But it's not important now, is it? I don't think the hit man had anything to do with the plane. It's a helluva coincidence—kill two birds with one stone and all—but he didn't do it."

Presley, suitably panicked, says "How can you be so sure?"

"I—I can't tell you that."

She sets her jaw. "*Can't?* Or *won't?*"

"Both."

She slaps him. Shouts, "What the fuck's the *matter* with you? Why would you *do* this to me?"

Mitch shrugs. "I thought you were having an affair."

"You couldn't *ask* me? We could have worked this out in a *conversation!*"

"I'm sorry," he says. I mean, I *know* you were having an affair. But...I shouldn't have done this. I'll find a way to make it go away."

"And if you can't?"

"I will. I'll just have to figure out how."

She grits her teeth. "You swear to God this is true? About the hit man?"

He nods. "I'm sorry."

"Then tell me everything, Mitch. If I mean anything to you at all, tell me what I need to know. Starting with why you don't think he did something to the plane. Like you said, it would be a way to kill me...and Ron...at the same time."

"He...the killer...offered me a discount...to let him rape you first. Before killing you."

Presley's head swirls. She barely manages to form the single word: "*What?*"

Mitch shrugs. "He said he could rape you *without* my permission, of course, but it would mean so much more if I agreed to it."

Presley can't focus her thoughts. If she *could*, she'd certainly wonder how the man she married—and slept beside every night—could authorize such a thing, and speak of it so casually. She pitches forward, feels herself losing consciousness, is vaguely aware her head has landed on her husband's arm. Hears him say something about how he doesn't think the hit man would have blown up the plane because he wanted to rape her first, and that clearly hasn't happened yet, so....

Seconds or minutes pass as Presley's brain seems to be operating in slow motion, as if clogged by a thick sludge. At some point she's conscious of a droning, low-volume alarm clock in the far distance. Hears people shouting, feels her torso being pulled upward from the bed, opens her eyes, sees Mitch's frozen stare, and realizes he's flat-lined.

Chapter 5

DANI RIPPER, PRIVATE INVESTIGATOR.

I'M SO STARTLED to hear that Fanny, our receptionist, has showed up for work, I nearly forget to take the call. But take it I do, only to hear some jerk impersonating an FBI agent: "Ms. Ripper?"

"Yes?"

"This is Agent Peterman, Federal Bureau of Investigation."

"Of course it is. What are you wearing, Agent Peterman?"

"Excuse me?"

"Let me guess: leather jacket, wife-beater tee, skinny jeans, Chukka boots?"

"This is no time for tom-foolery."

"It's not? How can you *say* that? Tom might be *exactly* who we need to get this party started!" My prank caller says nothing, so I step up to the plate with: "Try talking dirty. Ask about my milky thighs, or my dew-kissed honey mound. No? Then at least tell me this: boxers or briefs?"

The caller sighs. "Field agents adhere to a strict dress code. As you might expect, I'm dressed in accordance with standard protocol as befits a member of the Bureau."

"Are you wearing a watch chain? I can't abide a watch chain."

"How about we call it standard business attire, and move along to the serious issue at hand?"

"Serious? Are you *kidding* me? What on earth could be more serious than wardrobe? If it weren't for wardrobe, we'd all be naked. Are you imagining me *naked* right now? You *are*, aren't you!"

"No."

"When you say standard attire, do you mean red shirt and khakis, like Jake from State Farm, or cape and tights, like Batman and Robin? And where's your heavy breathing? I prefer heavy breathing from my crank callers."

"This is *not* a crank call! I'm an agent of the FBI, on official business, and—"

"You said your name was Agent Peterman. That's a lie right there."

"What are you *talking* about?"

"What sort of mother would name her child Agent? That's total bullshit. As for Peterman? I know a pornographic name when I hear one: *Peter-Man*? Oh, *please!*"

He hollers something about assuring me he's with the FBI, but I'd rather focus on the stunning, pale-eyed beauty who just entered my office. I hang up on Agent Peterman, or whatever his name is, and wave her in.

She approaches me nervously, and takes a seat.

I'd tell her how gorgeous she is, but that wouldn't be professional. If it were, I'd ask her what she eats, where she juices, and what she does to stay in shape. But since I can tell she's been crying long and hard, I slide a box of tissues across my desk and show my empathetic smile. As she summons the courage to tell her story, I think to myself:

> *I know exactly why you're here! Your wedding ring says you're married. Your clothes tell me you understand fashion, but can't afford the best, which tells me your husband's struggling to make ends meet. He's in sales, because how else could an average earner land a prize like you? He's a frustrated, petty little gnome, at least on the inside, who feels you slipping away, and senses it's more serious than merely distancing yourself sexually. He knows he doesn't deserve you and overcompensates by drinking too much and taking his frustrations out on you, and you're here for one reason only: because you're hoping I can dig up enough dirt on your husband to let you end this shitty marriage with dignity and a sense of outrage so you can tell your friends: "See what I've been living with? What I've had to deal with all this time? See what he's been up to?" This is why you're being forced to leave him, and not because Lance—*

the billion-dollar hedge fund manager you've been humping—has finally asked you to marry him.

She says, "Ms. Ripper, my name's Presley French, and I have reason to believe someone's planning to murder me."

"I knew it!" I say, clapping my hands, shamelessly. "The minute you walked in I said to myself, 'This woman's life has been threatened.'"

"You did?" she says, wide-eyed.

I smile. "I'm quite intuitive." I call Dillon, my teenaged computer-genius partner, and have him join us. After introducing him to Presley, I push my cell phone closer to her and press the record button. "Tell me everything."

Presley says, "I hope you've got plenty of memory on that thing."

"Are you kidding? It's got 128 gigabytes! Enough for 7,800 songs, 50 full-length movies...or one of Sophie's voicemail lectures."

"Sophie?"

"My girlfriend." I sit back in my chair and ask, "Who's planning to murder you?"

"I don't know his name, but he's a hit man."

I give her a look. "For real?"

She nods. "I think so."

"Tell me everything."

She does.

It's a lot to process.

Where to start?

I press a button to stop the recording, then get all of Presley's contact information, including what she can give me on Mitch's relatives. I give it to Dillon and say, "Start with Mitch's sister, then call his parents."

"Start...how?" Dillon says. "What do you want me to do?"

"Mitch cashed out his life insurance policy to pay the hit man. She doesn't know anything about the policy, and can't go home to search through Mitch's records, because it's the first place the hit man will look for her. So you need to call Mitch's sister, Chelsea. She and Mitch were very close and her husband *sells* insurance, so it's likely he sold Mitch the policy, and helped him cash it out. We're looking for anything you can get: who issued the policy, when did he cancel it, how much did he get?"

"How will that help us?"

"I have no idea. But it's good information to have."

"Why?"

"Because the more paper we produce, the thicker our files. And thick files not only help justify our fees, but can come in handy later on, if we're unable to find the bad guy."

"How?"

"On TV whenever the detective exhausts his very last lead, he sits at his desk and opens a thick file and turns a few pages and just before the last commercial break he notices something he never saw before."

"You think other people put stuff in the file when he's not looking?"

"No. It's always something that's been there from the first day, but this time he sees it differently. It's usually a photograph, but it can be anything. Since this is the first day, whatever we put in the file will probably be the thing that breaks the case later on."

"Um...You know Presley's listening to everything you're saying, right?"

I glance at her.

She lifts a hand from her lap and gives me a small wave.

"I knew that," I say.

"Okay, so I'll call Mitch's sister. What about his parents?"

"Presley's left messages, but hasn't heard from them. Maybe they'll take your call."

"What should I tell them?"

I notice Presley shaking her head no, so I say, "Never mind. Don't call the parents."

"Okay," Dillon says. "Just the sister.

"Wait!" I say.

"What now?"

"You can't call Chelsea."

"Why not?"

"We don't want to mention the hit man, because she might call the police."

"What's wrong with that?"

"I don't want them to know about the hit man."

"Why not?"

"Because they'll call the FBI, and the Feds will learn Presley didn't board the plane. Next thing you know they'll classify her as a suspected terrorist."

"So you want me to do what with all this information?"

"For now, just file it."

He shrugs his shoulders and leaves the room.

"We're more organized than we seem," I tell Presley. "This is just a really unique situation." As I press a button to dial the third name on my caller list I say, "But I have an idea."

After two rings, the most lethal person on the planet answers his phone: "Hey, Dani, what's up?"

"Donovan Creed!" I say. "How's married life?"

"For me or her?"

"Her."

"Heaven!"

I laugh. "I know you're busy, so I'll get to the point. Has someone hired you to kill a young lady?"

"Recently?"

"Yeah."

"Why do you ask?"

"Someone accepted a contract on my new client."

"Are you with her now?"

"Yes."

"Then it's not me."

"How do you know? I haven't even said her name."

"Think about it, Dani."

"Give me a hint."

"You said she's alive."

It takes a few seconds, then it comes to me: "If someone hired you to kill my client, she'd already be dead."

"That's right," Creed says. "I can't wait to hear your next question."

"What do you think it'll be?"

He laughs. "I think you're going to ask if there's some sort of secret network, or hired killer database your partner can hack into to find out who took the hit."

That's exactly what I was going to ask, but I wouldn't have phrased it so coherently. But since he's laughing about it, I say, "Don't be silly. I know there's no such database." I pause, waiting for him to comment. When he doesn't, I say, "Just to be clear, there *is* no such database, right?"

"You're too much!"

"Is that a no?"

"It is."

"If you were me, how would you go about locating this contract killer?"

"You sure you *want* to?"

"I'd like a chance to buy him off, if possible."

"So it's a man? You're sure?"

"Yes."

"Good. That makes it easier."

"Why?"

"Women are less likely to cancel a hit. They're better contract killers than men."

I pause a moment. "Are you joking with me?"

"No, but I can *tell* you an agency joke about this very subject. You ready?"

"Shoot."

"Okay, so a man and woman apply for a CIA assassin job. When the man comes in, the CIA Director says, 'Your wife is sitting in a chair in Room A, blindfolded.' He hands the man a gun and says, 'Go shoot her.' The man says, 'I can't do that!' The Director says, 'Then you don't get the job.' Then the woman comes in, and the director says, 'Your husband's sitting in a chair in Room B, blindfolded.' He hands her the gun and says, 'Go shoot him.' The woman takes the gun, goes in the room, and all hell breaks loose. When she comes out she says, 'The gun was filled with blanks, so I beat him to death with the chair.'"

I shake my head. "Charming."

"I never said it was a good joke. Who told your client it's a man?"

"Her husband."

"What's his name?"

"Mitch French."

"How would *he* know?"

"He's the one that hired the hit man. I'm putting you on speaker now, okay?"

"Okay," Creed says. "Who am I talking to?"

Presley looks at me.

I nod.

"Presley French," she says.

"Presley, don't be afraid. Dani will take good care of you. She's the best."

"Thanks," I say. "Any suggestions how to find this guy?"

"Saw one of Mitch's legs off."

Chapter 6

"MY HUSBAND'S DEAD," PRESLEY SAYS.

"Then saw the legs off his friends," Creed says. "Then his co-workers and family members. I guarantee someone will know *something*."

I frown. "We'd prefer to solve this case in a lawful manner, Donovan."

"You think this guy's planning to kill *Presley* in a lawful manner?" He sighs. "Ms. French, are you saying your husband *told* you he hired a hit man?"

"Yes," she says. "He told me this morning, before passing away. He had a seizure and knew he was going to die, and confessed everything. He said the killer's been following me, and I shouldn't visit my friends or family, or follow any type of regular routine."

Creed says, "What else did he say?"

"He said the hit man wanted to rape me first, then kill me."

"See? This is the sort of scum that's degrading our noble profession. I'm assuming you haven't been raped yet..."

When Presley fails to answer, Creed says, "*Have* you?"

Presley and I catch each other's eyes, hold our gaze...and she bursts into tears, which proves she *didn't* tell me everything a few minutes ago.

"I'll keep you posted!" I tell Creed, then hang up, come around my desk, hold Presley in my arms till she cries herself out.

"It didn't really hit me till just then," she says, between sniffs. "My husband's dead, and I've been raped."

"When did this happen?"

"Last night."

"You know the exact time?"

"What time did the plane blow up?"

"Five-forty."

"It was about fifteen minutes after that."

"Are these the clothes you were wearing?"

She nods.

"How many times have you used the bathroom?"

"I'm not sure. Twice, I think. I went straight to the hospital after it happened."

"Did they do a rape kit exam?"

"On *me*? No!"

"Why not?"

"I didn't tell anyone about it. Not even Mitch."

"Why?"

"Everything happened at the same time. I was supposed to be on the plane that crashed, but I never boarded because I broke up with the guy I was having an affair with."

"Why didn't you mention any of this a while ago?"

"I was more concerned about the hit man."

"You said you were having an affair."

She nods.

"Did your husband know?"

"He...yes. That's why he wanted to kill me."

"Tell me about the boyfriend. What's his name?"

"Doesn't matter. He's dead, too."

For a second I wonder how she could possibly lose her husband and her lover within twenty-four hours. Then it hits me: "Your lover was on the plane?"

"He was flying it."

"You were having an affair with the *pilot*?"

She nods.

"*Jesus*, Presley!"

She cries again, but softly. Then says, "My husband was injured by the wreckage from the plane. The police called to tell me he was being rushed to the hospital, but I didn't answer right away because I was in the middle of being raped."

"You...*what*?" I manage to say before being stunned into mouth-gaping silence, like Samantha, in *Sixteen Candles*, when she finds out Farmer Ted showed her underpants to the entire freshman class. Finally I ask, "Where were you raped?"

She gives me a strange look, then points at her crotch.

I shake my head and almost laugh, despite the seriousness of the subject. "I meant, where did the rape take place? In your car?"

"Oh. Midland Mall. In the parking lot."

"Details?"

"I went to the airport and sat at the gate, but didn't board. Ron—the pilot—was already on the plane, and couldn't say much, which was good, because I called and broke up with him just before takeoff. Then I left the airport, turned on my radio, and heard about the plane crash. All I could think was Ron had died moments earlier. I started convulsing, couldn't drive. Had to pull over, so I turned into the mall parking lot, got out of the car to clear my head, and the bastard attacked me. There were people all around, but no one even looked in my direction."

"Did you see his face?"

She nods.

"Seriously?"

She nods again. "And he took my wallet, so he knows where I live."

"In that case we need to do several things: first, tell me everything you can remember about the time prior to the assault. At the airport: who did you see that might have followed you? Who did you see in the airport parking lot? Did you notice anyone following you on the Interstate, or when you turned into the mall? Next, we'll do a rape kit. Then we'll contact a police sketch artist. Then we'll send the sketch to Donovan Creed. If this guy's the hit man, Creed will either know him, or know how to find him."

"What's a rape kit?"

"I'll tell you on the way to the hospital."

"Wait. I'm not sure I want to do that."

"Come anyway. I'll talk you into it while we drive. Trust me, it's essential."

"But—"

"What?"

"I haven't decided if I'm going to hire you yet."

"Too late. I'm already on the case."

"How much will this cost me?"

"I don't know yet. Somewhere between nothing, and whatever you can afford."

"There's not much difference between the two."

I laugh. "There never is. Can I drive you to the hospital now?"

"That depends."

"On what?"

Chapter 7

"WHAT'S A RAPE KIT?" PRESLEY ASKS FOR the second time.

I take a deep breath and say, "It's a collection of boxes, envelopes, plastic bags, microscope slides, stuff like that—used for collecting and storing evidence of the crime."

"Sounds like a big deal. I'm gonna say no."

"You *have* to do this, Presley!"

"They can't *make* me, can they? The police, I mean?"

"No, but it's something you *should* do, because the bastard who did this has probably done it before and will do it again. If your evidence puts him away, something good will have come out of this horrible situation. Other women will be that much safer because of you."

"Would *you* do it?"

"I *have* done it."

"Oh. I'm sorry."

"It's okay. We're not alone. One out of every four American women get raped during their lifetimes."

She gives me a look. "That can't be true."

"I'm afraid it is. And one of every five college girls will be sexually assaulted while pursuing her degree. It's a serious issue that isn't taken seriously enough."

She sighs. "How does this work? What would I have to do?"

"Give your medical history, any medications you're taking. They'll want all the details you can remember about the assault."

"What about the physical exam?"

"It's mostly samples. Clothing, hair, saliva, blood—that sort of thing."

"And?"

"And what?"

"Tell me the part you're sloughing over."

I try to sound casual while saying, "They'll check for semen and other bodily fluids, and make sure you haven't sustained any...uh...you know, injuries down there."

She frowns. "That sounds pretty invasive."

"It's not as bad as you think."

She arches a perfect brow. "Honestly, Dani?"

"Well, okay. It *is* as bad as you think. But it's super important to get tested. They'll offer you a morning-after pill and check for STDs."

Presley sighs again. "This isn't the guy who's planning to kill me, you know."

I say nothing.

"Dani?"

"Huh?"

"This isn't the guy. You know that, right?"

"Didn't Mitch say the hit man wanted to rape you first, then kill you? It *could* be him."

She arches that damn eyebrow again, and it's my turn to sigh. "You're right. The hit man and rapist are two different people. This was a totally random attack. He stumbled onto you at the mall, saw an opportunity, and took it. But you still need to do the rape kit....What's wrong?"

"I was hoping you'd disagree."

"I can't. Like Creed said, you're still alive. If a hit man wanted to assault you first, he'd do it in a secluded place, where he could control the situation. He wouldn't assault you in public, then run away and give you time to identify him."

Presley says, "It's probably too late for the rape kit. This happened last night."

"It's not too late. Immediately after is best, but rape kits can be effective up to 96 hours after an assault."

"Since he isn't the killer, maybe I should forget about the rape kit and find a safe place to stay."

"We need to do this, Presley."

"We?"

"I'll be right beside you, every step of the way. And afterward, you can crash with me and Sofe till we find you a better place."

"You'd better check with Sophie before making that offer."

"I will, but she'll say yes."

She's suddenly crying hard. It came out of nowhere.

"I'm sorry," she says, between sobs. "It's all...overwhelming."

I nod. "You're entitled."

She truly is. I'm dizzy just thinking about what she's been through in the past 16 hours: she broke up with her lover, who happened to be piloting the plane that crashed minutes after she decided not to board. The plane's remnants fell to the ground, hit her husband's car, and critically injured him. She left the airport, pulled into a mall parking lot...and was raped. Moments later, she rushed to the hospital to be by her husband's side, only to learn he paid a hit man to rape and kill her! Then her husband died! Any way you slice it, that's a bad day.

"Ready to go?" I ask.

"Okay."

As we walk from my office to the reception area, we notice my receptionist, Fanny, standing in the far corner, shaking her ass with more determination than a grade-schooler wiggles a loose tooth.

"*Excuse* us?" I say.

She turns around and says, "Oh, hi, Sugar! Whoa! You too, Wow Girl!"

If you don't know Fanny, you'll be surprised to learn this is her every day look. By choice. She shaves her head bald, and paints her head red.

Every morning.

From the base of her neck to the top of her forehead.

Bright red.

Don't Tell Presley!

And she's shapely. Think: more curves than the Santa Monica Freeway. And she sports tattoos on her ass that read, from left cheek to right: *If I'm drunk...Flip me over!*

Fanny says, "They were holding hands and dancing around the room like a fifties musical."

"Who was?"

"Jim and Slim."

"*Who?*"

"Our new clients. They waited for you till my phone rang, then started dancing to the tune, so I started dancing, and...I guess they danced right on out the door!"

Don't be alarmed by the horrific noise echoing through the room. That's not a spoon, caught in a garbage disposal. It's Fanny, laughing.

I'm serious, that's her laugh.

"What happened to Dillon?" I ask.

"I'm not sure. He was here a minute ago. Maybe he went to fetch Jim and Slim."

"Well, Jim and Slim will have to wait. Just to clarify, what we saw you doing in the corner just now: that was you, dancing?"

"What else?" She takes a few steps toward Presley, sees the tear stains on her cheeks. "You okay, hon?"

Presley nods.

"You need a place to stay tonight?"

"I've got it covered," I say.

Fanny winks. "I bet you *do!* Enough said. I got your back, boss lady. If Sophie finds out, it won't be *my* tongue that did the wagging, though this secret would be easier to

35

keep if my silence included a generous raise and some time off."

"Forget it," I say. "And for the record, we're not hiding anything from Sophie."

"Of course you're not!" Fanny says, giving us another wink.

Presley says, "I was sexually assaulted. Dani's taking me to the hospital for a rape kit exam."

Fanny says, "Oh. Sorry. All jokes aside, Dani will treat you right. She'll be more attentive than the horny couple in the Cialis commercial."

On the way to the hospital, Presley shocks me by saying, "We won't need the sketch artist."

"Why not?"

"I know who raped me."

I do a double-take. "You've seen him before?"

"I *know* him."

"From where?"

"He was my seventh-grade English teacher."

"No *shit?*"

"It was him."

"You're *sure?*"

She nods.

I say, "Scale from one to ten."

"Ten," she says.

I understand how rape trauma works. I've personally experienced it. Your eyes see something your mind doesn't always process *in the moment*. Even so, I'm surprised she's suddenly 100% certain about her attacker's identity. "That's fantastic! What's his name?"

Chapter 8

"JAMES QUELVIN," PRESLEY SAYS. WE CALLED HIM MR. Q."

"Did he recognize you?"

"Not even a little. But there's no reason he should have. It's been ten years since he saw me, and I was like twelve at the time."

"Why didn't you *say* something to him, or call him by name? He might have left you alone."

"I was afraid he might kill me if he thought I could identify him."

"Good point."

"I also needed time to be certain. In my mind."

"To process his face?"

"Yeah. It happened so fast, and I was totally stressed at the time. Not to mention it's been ten years for me, too, and he's aged a lot since seventh grade."

We drive a mile in silence before she says, "I guess we were right all along."

"About what?"

"We all thought Mr. Q. was creepy back then. Every day he wore white Keds with a business suit, and kept trying to sniff our hair."

"That *is* creepy. You grew up here in Nashville?"

"No, I'm from Tallahassee. That's another reason it took me so long to put it together. I wouldn't expect to see him here, except that..." Her voice trails off.

I give her a moment to complete her thought and it turns out to be a big one: "I thought I saw him here in town about a year ago."

"We're a long way from Tallahassee," I say. "Any chance you could be wrong?"

"About last year? Possibly. About last night? No. It was definitely Mr. Q. I'm 100% positive."

"Well, he should be easy to locate. There can't be many James Quelvins in Nashville."

"You're not taking me to Hailey Memorial, are you?"

"No. Why?"

"That's where Mitch died."

"Oh. Uh...Wow. I–"

"It's okay. I should have told you that earlier."

Unbelievable! Every now and again—too often, really– I'm reminded how stupid I can be! I didn't think to ask where he died. How awful would it have been for Presley if I took her to Hailey Memorial?

Jesus.

"I'm taking you to see a friend of mine, Doris Jones, at Metro General. Doris is a specially-trained Sexual Assault Nurse Examiner. She's really good. You'll like her."

"Is she the one who processed *your* assault?"

"I wish she *had* been! But no, they weren't very empathetic back in the day."

"How old were you?"

"Fifteen."

"I'm sorry."

"It's okay."

"If it was, you wouldn't be crying."

Am I crying?

I glance in the mirror.

Fuck.

"It really only gets to me when I see other people going through it. If you'd come into my office today with a different problem, I wouldn't be crying right now."

"I *did* come in with a different problem, remember? Someone's trying to kill me."

"Yeah, well I'm not going to let that happen."

We drive a few more minutes and pass a billboard advertising a scandalous movie that's currently playing in theaters.

"There are 256," I say. I can tell she has no idea what I'm talking about, so I explain: "The book says 50 shades of grey, but, according to Dillon, grayscale images are stored with 8 bits per pixel, which means there are actually 256 shades of grey."

I look at her for approval, but she says, "I'm not really sure how to respond to that."

"I only mentioned it in case it's been bothering you."

"Why would it bother me?"

The look on her face reminds me that most people aren't like me: they're normal.

We ride a few minutes in silence. Then she says, "Thanks for not judging me."

"What do you mean?"

"About the affair."

"I get it," I say. "I was married once."

Her eyes grow big. "You were?"

"Yup. And I fell in love with someone."

"Sophie?"

I nod. "It just sort of happened."

"Same here," she says. "I wasn't *miserable* with Mitch. It just...happened."

"How did it start with Ron?"

"I was going through a lot of stress at the time." She thinks a moment, then says, "Stress isn't the right word. I was living in fear. Maybe it's because he was older, but Ron made me feel safe."

"Why were you living in fear?"

She looks out the passenger window, but says nothing. So I say, "What made you end the affair?"

"Ron was all wrong for me."

"In what way?"

"He had his own demons. So I came to my senses and ended it. I felt Mitch deserved a better wife, figured maybe I should apply for the job."

We come to a stop light, and I ask, "Could you have been happy with Mitch after leaving Ron?"

Before she can answer, my phone rings. It's Fanny.

"What's up?" I say. "You're on speaker, by the way, so watch your language."

"Thanks for the warning. I hate to interrupt, but Jim and Slim finally showed up."

"What do they want?"

"They'd like you to contact their phone service provider and see if you can make them stop billing them for a phone they no longer have."

"Let me guess: the contract ended months or years ago, and the company won't let them cancel their monthly service without giving the password associated with the account, and they *know* the password, but some phone company moron entered it wrong in the system when the account was initially created, so every month the bills continue, even though they stopped using the phone months or years ago. And when Jim and Slim refuse to pay, the phone company turns it over to a collection agency."

"You got it."

"Dare I ask which company?"

She sighs. "It's the one whose name we're not allowed to mention."

"Cross yourself! Quickly!"

"I already did."

"The answer's no. You *know* how I feel about that bunch!"

"I do."

"Then why would you even entertain the thought?"

"We need the money."

"I'd rather sift through Satan's feces with my bare hands."

"You want me to tell them that?"

"No. It's not strong enough. Tell them I'd rather suffer eternal damnation and spend the rest of eternity tossing Satan's salad."

"Got it. Good thing you're watching your language."

"I know, right?"

When we get to Metro General, Doris greets Presley as if she's known her for years. She spends a few minutes chatting about her life, and her kids, and how she loves to cook, and where she's going on vacation this year. When she feels Presley's calm and relaxed, she says, "We're going to gather some evidence now, and I'm going to make the process as comfortable as possible."

"How long will this take?" Presley asks.

Doris pats her knee. "That's a good question! Most girls don't ask. But it'll depend on what kind of team we make. I've seen it take seven hours, and I've seen it take two. But if you and I can work together like I think we can, I'll have you out of here faster than you can watch *Titanic*. You ever seen that show?"

Presley nods.

"You like it?"

Presley shakes her head.

"Me either," Doris says. "But the song? Oh, I like that!" She smiles. "Okay, so before we get started, I want to make it clear you don't have to report this crime to the police if you don't want to, and you can refuse any part of the exam if you're uncomfortable with it." Then she looks around and whispers, "I'm required to say that, but I strongly urge you to see it through to the end, so we can get this criminal off the streets."

While Presley reads the consent form, I walk to the far corner of the room and text Dillon to find a current address for James Quelvin. By the time Presley signs the consent form, Dillon texts: *There's only one James Quelvin in the entire world, and he lives in Gatlinburg, Tennessee.*

Of course he does, because I hate Gatlinburg.

Chapter 9

"AM I PRETTY?"

"Aw shit," Sophie says. "What happened?"

Presley's in the exam room with Doris, giving her medical history, so I took this opportunity to call the person who knows me best.

Sophie asks, "Who said something, Dani? Who'd you see? Was it Erin? Shit. You saw one of her good photos somewhere, didn't' you!"

"I have no idea what you're talking about."

She sighs. "Why is it the prettiest women have the most issues?"

"Issues?" I say.

She laughs. "Okay, listen up, Dani, 'cause I'm only going to say this once: Erin Heatherton is drop-dead gorgeous. But she's only prettier than you in her *very*...best photos. The airbrushed ones. In real life she couldn't carry your makeup kit. She's got *freckles*, for God's sake!"

"Her freckles are adorable."

"Well...yeah, they are. But you're definitely prettier than she is."

"You think?"

"I know. Plus, she's freakishly tall. What is she, nine feet?"

"Six feet exactly."

"Oh. Well, she *seems* taller. But you're the perfect height."

"Thanks, Sofe."

"You're welcome. You're the fairest of them all, okay?"

"Okay. But it wasn't Erin."

"No?"

"New client. Presley French."

"Love the name!"

"I think she's prettier than me."

"That's impossible."

"She's crazy beautiful."

"Tell you what: give me two minutes in the same room under harsh lights, and I'll find every imperfection. What about her body?"

"Flawless, far as I can tell."

"No one's flawless. Ask where she works out. I'll take it from there."

"You can meet her in about an hour, if you'd like."

"What do you mean?"

"We're at Metro General."

"Hospital?"

"Yeah. With Doris Jones."

"Wait. You mean...? Aw, shit."

"I know. Poor kid."

"How old?"

"Twenty-two."

"This just happened?"

"Last night. But they'll want her clothes for the kit. Do you have time to gather some stuff and bring it?"

"When?"

"Now."

She sighs. "Yeah, I can do that. Is she your size or mine?"

"You and I are the same size."

"Yeah. In my *dreams*!"

"I think you're wrong about that. But my clothes should work," I say.

"I figured as much. What should I bring? Loose-fitting? Sweats?"

"Whatever you think. But...bring a hoodie and sunglasses, too."

"She's that badly beaten?"

"No, not at all. But someone's after her."

"The rapist?"

"A hit man."

Sophie goes quiet a long time before asking, "Surely you're not thinking about hiding her at our place, are you? Because the last time that happened—"

I cut her off, saying, "She has nowhere else to go."

"Funny thing about your clients: they never have anywhere else to go."

"Thanks, Sofe. Can you do me a favor?"

"Another one, you mean."

"Right. Can you call Sal?"

"Why?"

"Presley's husband, Mitch French, hired a hit man to kill her. Maybe Sal can ask around and find out who took the contract. If so, we might be able to get it canceled."

"Why would my uncle have any knowledge about those sorts of things?"

I want to say because he's the crime boss for the Midwestern United States, but I realize Sophie said that to warn me we're on cell phones and you never know who might be listening. So I say, "I was joking. Remember when we teased him about *Goodfellas*?"

"No."

"Oh. Well, maybe I was thinking of *my* uncle."

"You don't have an uncle."

"Right. Forget it. Bad joke."

Sofe says, "My uncle runs a wonderful charity. They do good deeds for deserving people."

"I know. The Mothers of Sicily. I've been there, remember?"

"Try to show some respect for my uncle's unwavering commitment to the needy."

"I will. Sorry. No more jokes. I promise."

"Last warning, okay?"

"Okay."

"Good. Because I love you, Dani, and I'd hate for Uncle Sal to cut your horse's head off and stick it in your bed."

"Not to mention I'd have to go out and buy a horse for him to kill."

Chapter 10

"CAFETERIA, FIRST FLOOR, BOOTH," I respond, when Sophie texts she just pulled into the hospital parking garage. As she approaches, I point to the hot chocolate I got her. This is the part where, if I were dating a guy, he'd say "Thanks," and that would be the end of it. But being a same-gender dating rookie, I've only just recently learned when you're dating a girl, everything has to mean something. Which is why Sophie's staring at the hot chocolate as if it might contain the key to the universe.

When she looks at my iced coffee, her facial expression makes it patently clear I've done something wrong, so I say, "Thanks for bringing the clothes. I know it came out of the blue, and it was really nice of you to drop whatever you were doing, and—"

"Whatever I was *doing?*"

"Your writing, I mean. I know it was an imposition."

"You're welcome. *And?*"

"And thanks for letting Press stay with us. Not many roommates—I mean, *girlfriends*—would do that."

"It's just for tonight, though, yes?"

"Uh huh."

"You're welcome." She arches an eyebrow. "Excuse me, but did you just say the word *Press?*"

I force myself not to take a deep breath, which is difficult, because even *I* can see what's coming.

I say, "She goes by Press sometimes."

"Is that what *you* call her?"

"I haven't yet."

"But you *want* to?"

I force myself not to roll my eyes. "I haven't really thought about it. I was just...that's her nickname."

"Did she *ask* you to call her Press?"

In my brain I'm screaming, *"For the love of God!"* But what I say is "No. She asked Doris to call her that, when they were getting acquainted."

"And that bothered you?"

"No."

"You're sure?"

I close my eyes a minute. Hell, maybe it *does* bother me! Maybe I'm jealous she asked Doris to call her Press, and not me. I mean, I don't *think* it bothers me, or at least, I'm pretty sure it *didn't* bother me till just now!

Should it bother me?

This is what it's like dating a woman. They—should I say *we?*—scrutinize every detail. Parse every comment for context and hidden meanings. I feel like I can do things with the best intentions, things I consider thoughtful and utterly selfless, and in the space of a single word, wind up looking like an insensitive boob.

Don't get me wrong, there are a million benefits to dating a woman. I'm just saying...

Sometimes it's exhausting.

You have to dress well all the time, or at least appropriately for every occasion...and *everything's* an occasion! Staying up late and gossiping about our mutual friends is an occasion (funny pajamas). Sunday morning sleep-ins are an occasion (blue panties, Titans jerseys). Monday night TV *Bachelor* parties are an occasion (clothing varies weekly, based on theme). Examining and constantly re-examining our relationship is an occasion (clothing range: naked to elegant, as this can take place in any setting, at any time, without warning. Including hospital cafeterias).

Sophie says, "You're drinking iced coffee."

I nod. "Want a sip?"

"No thanks."

"Want to trade?"

"Nope."

"What's wrong?" I say, knowing she'll say "Nothing."

"Nothing," she says. "Why do you ask?"

"Because you're looking at me funny."

"I was just wondering if drinking iced coffee in the winter might be the equivalent of taking a cold shower."

"I have no idea what that means."

"Allow me to recap: you were in the exam room with a gorgeous young lady you think is prettier than *you*, which makes her *far* prettier than me. From what I understand, rape exams are quite revealing."

"I didn't see her body or anything."

"You're sure?"

"Positive. She kicked me out before undressing."

"And that bothered you?"

"Of course not."

"And yet you went straight from the exam to the cafeteria and ordered iced coffee."

"So?"

"In winter."

I frown. "We're in Nashville. You see anyone wearing a jacket outside?" I put my hand on hers. "You don't have to worry about Presley. She's as straight as Bruce Jenner."

"What is that, some sort of *joke?*"

"What do you mean?"

"Have you not seen the photos?"

"Of what?"

"Bruce Jenner. They're saying he wants to be a woman."

"*Who's* saying that?"

"*Everyone!* Jesus, Dani, where have you *been?*"

Now I sigh.

Deeply.

Like I said, I'm new at this whole same-gender relationship dynamic, and it can be tiresome. On the other hand, we get to have picnics and parades.

Sophie says, "I'm just wondering what all this says about our relationship."

Of course she is. "Should I have ordered a hot chocolate?"

"Not if you were horny."

"I'm horny for *you*, Sofe."

"Oh, great. Thanks a lot!"

"What now?"

"You're horny for me by default!"

"*What?*"

"You spent hours of quality, highly-emotional time bonding with...*Press*. By the time the private exam started, you were all worked up to the point she felt uncomfortable letting you see the good stuff."

"*Good* stuff?"

"You know what I'm talking about: you wanted to see her body, and she wouldn't let you. So you left the room, went straight to the cafeteria to order your cold shower drink. At some point you remembered I was coming, so you defaulted me to the fat girl's drink, the hot chocolate."

"You *love* hot choc—"

—"And you're suddenly horny for *me*? Well, gosh, thanks, Dani! But if so, it's only because you were horny for *her*, and she's not interested. Since I am, I suppose I'm better than nothing, but I hardly think...that *you* think...that—"

"*Stop!*" I yell. "*My head's about to explode!*"

Sophie's eyes are wide as water lilies. "Lower your *voice!*" she hisses, angrily. Mortified by the "scene" I just caused, she looks down at the table and covers both sides of her face with her hands.

I say, "Sofe? You don't have to hide the right side of your face. We're sitting by the wall."

"Fuck you."

I take a deep breath, let it out slowly. "I'm sorry I embarrassed you—I mean *us!*—just now. I'm sorry about everything I did wrong. I thought you *liked* hot chocolate. I thought it was your beverage of choice. I thought the temperature of the drink would help alleviate your concerns about the germs on the hands of the cafeteria workers. I thought meeting in the cafeteria would make you feel less vulnerable to airborne diseases than being in the lobby or hallways. I know how brave and difficult it was for you to even get out of your car in the hospital parking lot, not to mention *enter* the hospital, and I was trying to be as thoughtful as possible about your germ phobia. I thought of buying you a little stuffed bear from the gift shop, but even *I* was afraid to touch it!" I pause, then add, "I can't tell you how grateful I am that you brought a change of clothes for Presley, and I'm sure she'll be extremely grateful, too. She's a decent person, Sofe, and doesn't deserve the shit that's happened to her."

I sigh, then add, "And I'm sorry I didn't know Bruce Jenner wants to be a woman, though I'm not positive that's true—or I would've come up with a better example of how straight Presley is. But her being straight doesn't matter. And her looks and your looks don't matter. What matters is our relationship, which I thought was perfect…until you walked into the cafeteria just now."

We look at each other a minute. Could she possibly need more reassurance?

She could, and does.

So I say, "And my drinking iced coffee has nothing to do with wanting to see Presley's woo hoo. I just felt like having iced coffee, as I often do when I'm stressed, which tends to happen whenever I'm exposed to rape victims, since they remind me of what happened to me all those years ago. So anyway, I'm sorry about the iced coffee and hot chocolate, and I'm sorry I made you jealous by saying Presley was gorgeous. The reason I told you that is because I knew she was coming to spend the night with us, and I was worried you'd find her more attractive than me."

Sophie finally speaks: "Thank you."

"For what?"

"Saying enough of the right things to reassure me."

"And the hot chocolate?"

"You got it exactly right without asking."

"Does that mean you and I are okay?"

"I hope so. Where's Presley?" she says.

"She kicked me out of the room when Doris informed her it was time for her speculum exam."

Sophie laughs. "Straight women, right?"

"She's been through a lot, Sofe."

"I didn't mean to sound insensitive," she says, "I was just—"

"I know. Keeping it light. I'm the same way."

"Actually, I'd say you're inappropriate. Most of the time, anyway."

"Thanks."

She laughs.

"What?"

"Did you actually say those three words a few minutes ago?"

"Probably. Which ones?"

"Presley's *woo hoo*?"

I smile.

She smiles.

All this to get back where we were before she showed up.

While she sips her drink I think about how Presley's eyes got wide when she saw Doris reaching for the speculum. "You have to leave now, Dani!" she said.

"I promised to stay with you the whole time," I said.

"And you have. But now it's time to leave. I'll call you when we're done."

"Is this because you think I'm gay?"

"Yes. That's exactly the reason," Presley said.

"*What? Seriously?*"

"No, of course not. I only said that because it was a stupid question. The truth is I barely know you, and we just started a professional relationship. Would you bring your real estate agent to your gyno exam and let her sit by the stirrups?"

"Good point. But—"

"How about your dentist?"

"Nope, but—"

"Your attorney?"

"You're right. I'll check back in a few."

"Check back when I call you."

"Okay. Got it."

As I walked out the door she hollered, "You didn't happen to mention the speculum exam!"

She's right. Nor did I mention the pubic hair pull, the anal swabs, or the colposcope photos Doris will take to check for genital injury.

Sophie says, "How long till she's done?"

"Thirty minutes, give or take. You want to stay and meet her?"

"I need to pick up stuff for the party tonight. We're still on, right?"

I look at my watch. "Sure. Wouldn't miss it."

"You know what we're talking about, right?"

"The Bachelor?"

"Wow, I'm impressed! When are you bringing her home?"

"After we file the police report."

"How long will that take?"

"Couple hours."

"What about personal items?"

"We'll swing by the drug store and get whatever she needs."

"So you'll be home by what, five-thirty?"

"Six at the latest. How many are coming tonight?"

"Including *Press*? Nine."

"What happened to the others?"

"Vandy's at home tonight."

"Again?"

"That's my understanding."

"They'd rather watch basketball than *The Bachelor*?"

"No, but their husbands have season tickets."

I frown. "Straight women, right?"

She rolls her eyes. "A for effort, but you're not quite there yet."

"Gayness is tricky," I say.

"Hang in there. You'll get it."

"How long does basketball season last?"

"Forever. You think Presley will be up for the party tonight?"

"Let's not give her a choice. It'll be good for her."

Chapter 11

AS I ENTER THE POLICE STATION and see Officer Vic Mix approaching, I remind myself to keep my "fucking mouth shut," as if I'm sharing an elevator with Ray Rice. As he closes in, I motion Presley to hang back.

"When are you gonna flash me that gorgeous smile of yours?" Vic says.

"At your funeral."

"Hilarious." He suddenly spots Presley: "Holy *shit!* Who's *that?*"

"Never mind. Where's Christine?"

"Downstairs. I can get her if you like."

"Please do."

When he fails to move, I say, "I'm here to file a police report. Are your shoes stuck to the floor, or…"

"I've never seen two women this pretty at the same time!" he says. He motions Presley to come closer. She takes two tentative steps forward, then stops. Vic extends his hand

and says, "Officer Vic Mix at your service. Who're you, Darling?"

Presley looks at me like a puppy that's fallen into the deep end of a swimming pool, and can't get out.

I show Vic my hard stare: "Your tongue's hanging out, Vic. I don't blame you, I wouldn't want that nasty thing in my mouth, either. But show a little restraint, will you?"

He ignores me and says, "You may as well tell me your name, Sugar. I'll get it off Christine's report anyway," he says.

"That's not gonna happen," I tell Presley, but now she's looking around the station room and sees all eyes staring her down.

She starts shaking.

"Dani, I—I can't do this."

"Do what, Sugar?" Vic says.

I scowl at him. "Thanks a lot, asshole."

"Hey!" he says, defensively. "I'm just trying to be friendly. What's *your* problem?"

"At the moment? Sexual harassment."

I take Presley's arm and start leading her back to the hall. Vic jumps in front of us to block our path. He lowers his voice, but spits the words with great menace: "This wasn't harassment. You *understand?*"

It's supposed to be a secret, but I happen to know Vic's on his way out of the police department. It's down to the lawyers and paperwork. But since his lawyers are fighting to save his pension, I'd prefer not to be the reason he loses it. Which is why I'm holding my tongue.

Presley, on the other hand, widens her big blue eyes and says, "You're a cop, Vic?"

His anger melts like ice in a microwave. "That's right, Sugar."

"So where the *fuck* were you last night when I was being *raped at the mall?*"

"Keep your voice down!" he warns.

Presley says, "You'd better haul ass, Vic, 'cause I'm about to let loose the scream of the tenth apocalypse."

Vic isn't sure he believes her, but when she takes a deep breath and rolls her eyes up in her head he backs away from us like we're the hotel twins from *The Shining*.

We finally meet Officer Christine Herold, who works in Sex Crimes, which is part of the Investigative Services Bureau. Christine tries to talk Presley into having me wait outside during the interview, saying they can do their job a lot more efficiently without my interference, but Presley insists I be included, which is why Christine can be seen rolling her eyes at me.

It's okay, I'm used to police hate.

I don't always solve the cases they can't, but I've had several notable successes with suspects they'd ruled out that made the national news, so they tend to regard me as the enemy. The good news is I have a couple of high-ranking friends in the department who contact me privately when their investigations hit a wall.

Though Christine dislikes me, I have to admit she does an excellent job of interviewing Presley. After asking a wide array of questions, she has her write a detailed account of the assault, then records Presley's statement about recognizing her assailant as James Quelvin, her former English teacher, from Tallahassee.

"My partner did a trace on Mr. Quelvin," I say. "He's living in Gatlinburg."

"I'll take that with a grain of salt and throw it over my shoulder," Christine says.

"If Dillon says he's located him, you can take it to the bank," I say, defensively.

"Have you spoken to a rape counselor yet?" Christine asks.

"Doris Jones," Presley says.

"Doris is more like a nurse than a rape counselor. I'd like you to talk to one of our specialists before you leave."

"I'd rather not," Presley says.

Christine sighs. "I can't force you, but I strongly urge you to reconsider. You're putting a brave face on it, but I can assure you this assault will have an effect on you."

"I understand. But I'd rather not."

"May I ask why?"

"Because the rape is the least of my problems."

Presley and I exchange a look, but Christine's already asking, "What do you mean?"

I don't want Presley telling the police about the hit man for a number of reasons, but mainly because her story will reveal two details that could make her a suspect in the plane crash: (1) she was dating the pilot, and (2) she was scheduled to board but changed her mind at the last minute. That information would cause the police to call the FBI, and Presley's world would suddenly turn into a shit show. Her rape will take a back seat to the terror investigation, and she could wind up in federal prison if the FBI determines someone tampered with the plane and can't figure out who. Not only that, but Donovan Creed and Sal Bonadello are already asking around to see who in their community of killers might have accepted the hit. If it's a credible threat, either of these men could diffuse it quickly. But Sal's help comes with a caveat: if he learns the police or FBI are involved, he'll distance himself from the whole affair, and we'll lose a major asset.

Presley recovers nicely on her own, saying, "I just meant I'd like to take a raincheck. I'm exhausted."

"She's been through a lot already," I say.

Christine looks at her like she's seen it all, and Presley's rape is as tame as it gets. Then again, she doesn't know about Presley's affair, the plane crash, the dead lover, the dead husband, or the hit man. To Presley she says, "When do you think you'll make your decision about prosecuting?"

"Soon," Presley says.

"Very well." She hands Presley a card. "Here's Mary Delaney's contact information. She's our top counselor. Mary can help you process what's happened, and help you move forward. Please call her tomorrow."

"Okay."

"In the meantime we'll try to locate Mr. Quelvin." She looks at me. "Wherever he might be."

"Gatlinburg," I say.

"We'll be in touch," she says.

"What about the rape kit?" I say.

"We'll collect it from Mrs. Jones, and test for DNA. If we find something we'll enter it into CODIS."

"What's that?" Presley asks.

"The national FBI database that tracks serial offenders. If we get a match—"

"It's Mr. Quelvin," Presley says.

I tell Christine, "You should get a sample of Mr. Quelvin's DNA."

"Thanks for telling me how to do my job."

I give her a look. "You don't like me, do you?"

"I don't. But it's not personal."

"How can it not be personal?"

"Fine. It's personal."

"Presley's my client, and I'd like to think your personal feelings about me won't have an impact on your efforts."

"You can think whatever you want," Christine says.

"Thanks for giving me permission. What I think is, if you were on *The Bachelor*, you'd never get the first impression rose."

Chapter 12

YOU'RE RIGHT," SOPHIE SAYS. "SHE IS PRETTIER THAN YOU!"

"Excuse me?"

Sophie shrugs. "It's close, but she gets the nod. I couldn't find anything wrong with her. She's flawless."

We're home, setting up for our Monday night get-together. Presley's in the guest shower getting cleaned up. "What flaws do *I* have?"

"None. You're flawless too."

"That can't be true, or you wouldn't have put her above me. And anyway, I thought you were my friend."

"I'm your best friend in the world. *And* your lover."

"Then you should lie, to make me feel better."

"I would, but I know how much you value honesty."

I set my jaw. "Go ahead, get it all out now, before she comes out of the shower all cleaned up and even more beautiful. I don't want her to see me pout. It makes my eyes look squinty."

"I'm not trying to be mean," she says.

"Rate her. Scale of one to ten."

"She's off the charts, Dani. This is literally the prettiest woman I've ever seen."

"Prettier than Callie Carpenter?"

"*No* one's prettier than Callie Carpenter!"

I frown. "So now I'm *third* in your eyes?"

Sophie sighs. "Let me ask you a question: what do you think of my songwriting abilities?"

"You're my favorite songwriter in the whole world!"

"Thanks. But am I the *best* songwriter in the whole world?"

"To *me* you are."

"Thanks again. Now tell the truth. Pretend you don't know me. Pretend we're not dating. Isn't it possible there are at least ten better songwriters in the world?"

"No."

"Dani?"

"Fine. It's possible. But they're probably totally fucked in the head."

She laughs. "They *definitely* are! But the point is, there's always someone prettier than we are, or better at whatever we do best."

"*That's* supposed to cheer me up?"

"Nope. I've got something far better."

"Let's hear it."

"Brace yourself."

"Okay. I'm braced."

"This is really big."

"So *tell* me already!"

"Presley thinks you're prettier than she is."

"*What? Seriously?* You're *sure?*"

"She told me so."

"No way!"

"I swear."

"How did she say it, exactly?"

"She thanked me for letting her stay here, and for getting Uncle Sal to help her find the hit man. At some point I asked her what she thought about you, and she said you were the most gorgeous woman she's ever seen."

"She said that?"

"She did."

"Those were her exact words?"

"Yup."

"Well, that's nice of her to say. I hope you told her I don't place much emphasis on my looks."

"Of course."

"Thanks, Sofe."

Chapter 13

"OMIGOD, I CAN'T WAIT!" one of our guests squeals.

ABC's *The Bachelor* is sort of like *Lord of the Flies*, except with chicks and liquor. And tonight's a big night for our Monday night group, since it's *The Women Tell All* episode.

"We probably won't drink as much tonight as we usually do," I tell Presley.

"Why not?"

"Tonight's a recap of the season. But it's still our favorite show each year because the former contestants trash each other like crazy. There'll be lots of tears. By the way, if your character cries, you have to pay everyone a dollar and drink a shot of whiskey."

"So you've turned *The Bachelor* into a drinking game?" she says. "How does it work?"

"Before the season starts we put the contestants' names in a hat and take turns drawing till they're all accounted for.

For each woman you draw, you put $5 in the pot. If your woman wins the season, you get the pot."

"How does the drinking part work?"

"Every time someone says the word 'amazing' everyone has to curse, put a dollar in the pot, and drink a shot of whiskey."

"Does that happen very often?"

"Let me put it this way: no one shows up without a designated driver."

"*The right reasons*," Sophie prods.

I laugh. "Right! I forgot to mention the dare sock. We write dares on pieces of paper. If one of your women says the phrase 'the right reasons' we all have to pay you $5 out of our pockets, but if you want to keep the money you have to pull a dare from the sock and do it in front of everyone during the next commercial. If you refuse, the person who wrote the dare gets the money but has to do the dare."

"What are the dares?"

"We're not allowed to say, but you can bet several of us will be doing dares tonight, when the cat fights start, since they always accuse each other of not being on the show for the right reasons."

"Sounds like fun."

"Wanna play?"

"Sure."

Sofe and I smile and give her a big hug. Then I give her one of the names I drew at the beginning of the season. Within an hour Presley's having a ball, carrying on like a pro, shouting, "*Omigod!* Tell me that girl didn't just strip naked in front of the whole world and jump in the water! Her *parents* are watching!"

Everyone laughs.

"*Omigod!*" she says later. "Could you ever get that *drunk?*"

Afterward she says, "I had no idea watching a TV show could be so much fun!"

"We start the show and trust the liquor," I say. "It gets pretty crazy."

Presley says, "You're right about how often they say 'amazing.' The *town* was amazing, the *dinner* was amazing. Even those nasty little *monkeys* were amazing!"

I say, "They can't help themselves. If these guys on The Bachelor think the *potato salad* is amazing, what will they say if someone invents a cookie that can make them immortal?"

She laughs. "You guys are crazy!"

"No," Sophie says, "We're *amazing!* And you are, too."

The next morning Christine Herold, from Sex Crimes, calls and says, "Tell your client we've ruled out James Quelvin as a suspect."

"What do you mean?"

"She got it wrong."

"Which part?"

"All of it. He didn't do it."

"You're saying he has an alibi?"

"I'm saying he didn't do it. And that's all I'm going to say."

"You can't have checked the mall security cameras this quickly."

"Don't need to. Not for Quelvin."

"Why not?"

"He wasn't there."

"How can you be so certain?"

"Figure it out for yourself."

"Excuse me?"

"Why should I do your job for you?"

"Uh...because a girl's been *raped*? And we're on the same *team*?"

"We're not on the same team, Ms. Ripper. And your client has major credibility issues."

"Fine. Don't tell me. But you *are* planning to pull the mall tapes, right?"

"Probably not."

"You can't be serious!"

"Mall security says the cameras aren't effective where Ms. French claims the assault took place."

"Why not?"

"If she's to be believed, she was far closer to the street than the mall. At that distance the cameras don't show enough detail for a positive ID."

"Maybe not, but they'd show the attack."

"If you're looking for proof of the attack, I'd say *you're* starting to question your client's story."

"That's not even remotely true, Christine. My client says the rapist ran away after the assault. Since she was facing the street, he could only have run in two directions: parallel, or back toward the mall. If parallel, the cameras might have caught him getting into his car. Even at that distance we should be able to get make, model, and color. And if he ran *toward* the mall he may have gotten close enough for the cameras to give us a positive ID. Either way, we need to review them."

"Surprisingly, you've made a good point. But I can't justify the man hours necessary to build a case she may not be willing to prosecute. Personally, I think she's hiding something."

"Like what?"

"Are you aware her husband died yesterday?"

"Of course."

"You think that's a coincidence?"

"You think it *wasn't*? A plane crashed! Presley's husband isn't the only person who died from the wreckage. So far we're up to what, sixty dead?"

"Sixty-two and counting. But how many of *their* spouses claimed they were raped?"

"If I said *all* of them, *that* would be a coincidence."

"Just so you know, we're considering an autopsy on Mitch French."

"Why the hell should *I* care?"

"Your client might, if she's got something to hide."

"You can't possibly think she killed her husband."

"Why not? He was in stable condition when the nurse left the room, and Ms. French was alone with him when he died."

"Yeah, that's probably never happened in a hospital before: a wife being alone in the room when her husband passed away. I worked a case where a woman fell out of her hospital bed and was knocked unconscious. They didn't find her until three hours later, when an intern and a volunteer student tripped over her body while consummating their crush."

"That sounds like a personal anecdote. Were *you* the volunteer student?"

She hangs up, leaving me to stare at my phone till Presley asks, "What's wrong?"

"Is there anything you need to do today?"

"You mean like funeral arrangements?"

"Yeah."

"I'm not feeling it. Why?"

"Wanna come with me to Gatlinburg?"

"Would I have to confront Mr. Q?"

"No."

"Are *you* going to?"

"Yes. But *you* don't have to see him."

"In that case, I'll go."

"Have you heard from Mitch's parents yet?"

"Nope, and I don't expect to. They've always hated me."

"Because of the affair?"

"Well, now that you mention it, if Mitch knew about the affair as long as he claimed, I'm sure he told Selma, since he was quite the mama's boy. But no, his parents hated me from day one."

"The mom's name is Selma?"

She nods.

"*Selma?*" I repeat.

"Yes. Why?"

"That's a terrible name. She's got a *right* to hate people. Starting with her *own* parents."

"Well, if anything good can be said to come out of Mitch's death, not having to deal with Selma, Bass, and Chelsea tops the list."

"Did you say Bass? Like the fish?"

"Yeah, but that's not his real name. It's what he wants people to call him."

"What's his real name?"

She smiles. "I *knew* you were gonna ask me that. I've got to think a minute. All I've ever called him is Bass. Selma and Bass."

"How bad could a man's name possibly be that he prefers to be called the name of a fish? I can see it now: 'Mom and Dad? I want you to meet my new boyfriend, Flutterbutt. Please call him Swordfish.'"

She looks at me with great curiosity, like in *The Princess Bride*, when Westley looked at the Albino before being tortured in the Pit of Despair.

"George," she says.

"Huh?"

"That's Bass's real name."

"*George?*"

She nods.

"Go figure. So what about the funeral arrangements?"

"Selma's a control freak. She'll be thrilled I'm not there. That way she can handle everything." She pauses. "You want to know how much they hate me? They didn't even call me back when I left the message that Mitch died."

"You *voice mailed* them their son died?"

"I didn't know what else to do! They wouldn't answer my calls. Even when I left the message about his seizure they never got back to me. And I knew the hospital wouldn't tell them he died. Not over the phone, anyway. I figured they'd want to know. I mean, even if you hate your daughter-in-law, wouldn't you want to comfort her when her husband's been in a car wreck, and suffered a seizure?"

"I would. It's very peculiar, and I honestly don't know what to make of it. But speaking of the funeral, if you want to attend, I should probably arrange for protection."

"I'm not going."

"You're sure?"

"The whole family hates me, and Mitch hired someone to *kill* me! Then, to save a few bucks, he told the killer he could *rape* me first! His own *wife*! The only reason I'd go is to hike up my dress and piss on his casket, but it would be rude to do that at his funeral."

"We can save it for later. I'll take you."

"Thank you, Dani." She smiles. "Don't let me forget."

I pull out my phone, press the note page icon, and dictate: "After the funeral, when everyone's gone, take Presley to the cemetery to piss on Mitch's grave!"

Chapter 14

ON THE WAY TO GATLINBURG I call Dillon and ask, "What have you got for me?"

"What do you mean?"

"James Quelvin."

"What about him?"

"What did you find out?"

"I already told you. There's only one, and he lives in Gatlinburg."

"That's *it*? That's all you could *find*?"

"You asked me to find James Quelvin. I found him and gave you his address and phone number. What else did you want?"

"*Jesus*, Dillon!"

"What?"

"On TV, the detective says what, five words of dialogue? Like, 'Get me the Jarsdale File!' -And within seconds, the nameless assistant produces a thin file with an unbreakable rubber band wrapped around it that contains everything the detective needs to solve the case."

"*Jarsdale* File? Nameless assistant?"

"You know what I mean."

"Well, I can *do* all those things—except for the rubber band—if you think to *ask* me first."

"You're supposed to *know!*"

"Is this about Gatlinburg?"

"No. Yes. I mean, what do you know about Gatlinburg?"

"I know your uncle put you on a roller coaster ride when you were a kid and you peed your pants."

"Who *told* you that?"

"You did, that time you were trying to comfort me when I thought I was gonna get laid and didn't. And later, I told you about the lady in Florida who married a Ferris wheel, remember?"

I laugh. "She used to feed it pizza, right?"

"That's right. True story."

"You know what, Dillon? There are a lot of crazy people running around."

"Remember that today, and be careful."

"You too." I pause. "You know I love you, right?"

"Yeah. I hope so, anyway."

"Well, I do."

"Okay."

"Dillon?"

"What?"

"Say it. Tell me you love me too."

"It's weird to say that. And anyway, you're on speaker."

Presley looks over at me and smiles.

"I'm on the *highway*, Dillon! I could get hit by a tractor trailer any minute. Think how awful you'd feel if I died and you didn't tell me you love me."

While he's saying: "I'll take my chances," I catch Presley's eye and whisper "Scream on three!" I hold up one finger, a second, then...she and I scream bloody murder, and I hang up the phone.

Seconds later he calls me back, but I don't answer. So he texts: *Are you sure you're not my mom?*

When I call him back he says, "Want me to run a complete profile on James Quelvin?"

"Yes, please."

"Should I put that at the top of my list?"

"Yup."

"Okay. Sorry I didn't think to do it yesterday afternoon."

"It's all right. I should have told you."

"By the way, you used six words."

"When?"

"You said, 'What have you got for me?' –That's six words, not five, like the detectives on TV."

"Oh. Well no wonder you didn't know what I meant."

Over the next two hours I mentally rehearse all the questions I plan to ask James Quelvin when he answers his front door. But when I get there and see him, only one of my questions is relevant: "Are you James Quelvin?"

"Yes," he says. "And you're the one who called a little while ago? Dani Ripper?"

I'm so stunned by his appearance I can barely nod.

He says, "You drove all the way from Nashville?"

I nod again.

"Why?"

"Sir?"

"The police already checked my alibi, didn't they?"

I nod.

"Well?"

"Huh?"

"Was there a problem with it?"

"You're James Quelvin?"

"I still am."

"Can you prove it?"

"Do I need to?"

"No. But it would make my job a lot easier."

He pulls his wallet from his hip pocket, shows me his driver's license.

"Thanks," I say. "I'm sorry to take up your time."

"No problem. I was just surfing the Web."

He closes the door, locks it.

I remain on his porch staring straight ahead, trying to regroup. After a minute or two, I knock again.

"Yes?"

"You don't by chance have a twin brother, do you?"

"Nope."

"A close cousin with similar features?"

"Nope."

"Friend of the family who resembles you?"

"You're being too polite, Ms. Ripper. Why don't you just ask if my parents ever had a child they gave up for adoption?"

"Did they?"

"Not to my knowledge, but it should be easy enough to research."

"How so?"

"There weren't many Quelvin's running around in the 1970s, and my mother's maiden name was Nithercott, which is so rare as to be nearly extinct. A quick check of birth records from that decade should tell you what you need to know."

"Not necessarily. Your father could have had a one-night stand and impregnated a woman who didn't know his last name. If so, she couldn't have named him as the boy's father on the birth certificate."

"You came up with that on the fly? I'm impressed! But the odds are against it."

"Why's that?"

"My father died in a car crash at the age of sixteen."

"That's pretty convenient, don't you think?"

"You think my father purposely died forty years ago just so he could confuse you today?"

"Are you sure he fathered *you*?"

"Isn't that the very definition of a father?"

"Yes, but the fact he raised you doesn't make him your birth father."

"I can see why you're a detective. Perhaps you should have been an attorney."

"Bite your tongue!"

He laughs. "Far as I know, he was my birth father, and I find it hard to believe my mom would lie about it."

"Why?"

"She said he got her pregnant when they were both fifteen, and he died two months before I was born. And before you ask if my mom had any other children after I was born, the answer is an emphatic no. Shortly after I was born she contracted a pelvic infection that rendered her infertile."

"And you've been…uh…like *this* for how long?"

"Four years."

"Again, Mr. Quelvin, thanks for your time."

"Glad to help. Good day."

He closes the door for the second time, and locks it. I start walking to my car, then stop. Thirty seconds later I'm knocking on his door again.

"What now?" he says.

"Do you happen to have any personal photos from approximately ten years ago?"

"I'm sure I do. Why do you ask?"

"I wonder if I could see one."

He sighs. "Is it important?"

"It could be."

"Okay. You want to come inside or wait out here?"

"I'll wait out here."

A few minutes pass before he opens the door. When he does, he hands me two photographs. I study them a minute, then stare at his face. "These are you?"

He nods.

"You know when they were taken?"

"Approximately ten years ago. Isn't that what you asked for?"

"It is, thank you."

"Anything else?"

"When did you leave Tallahassee?"

"What do you mean?"

"Ten years ago you were teaching English in Tallahassee. At some point you left. What year was that?"

"I never taught school in Tallahassee."

"Excuse me?"

"I've never taught school in Tallahassee, or anywhere else. I'm a diesel fitter by trade."

"You're certain?"

He says, "Can I ask you a question?"

"Sure."

"Have *you* ever taught school in Tallahassee?"

"No."

"Are you certain?"

We stare at each other till I say, "Point taken."

"Thank you."

"So you *are* certain?"

He laughs. "I am. Can I have my pictures back?"

"Oh. Sorry. I thought they were for me."

"Would you like to keep one?"

"Yes."

"Take your pick."

I choose one and hand him the other. "Thanks for seeing me, Mr. Quelvin."

"My pleasure. Should I wait a few minutes before closing my door?"

"No. I'm done. Thank you."

He stands there anyway, till I back completely out of his driveway, then waves goodbye, and shuts his door.

Two miles later I pull into the parking lot of the McDonalds where I left Presley. Thankfully, she's inside, and alive.

"I *told* you no one would shoot me in here," she says.

"You did, and I'm grateful. Did you turn your phone on?"

"No, but it wasn't easy."

"Good girl."

"You really think the killer could be tracking my cell phone?"

"No. But it would be bad for business if he proves me wrong and kills you."

"How did it go with Mr. Q?"

"He's not the guy."

"What are you *talking* about? Of *course* he's the guy! I got a good look at him, remember?"

I pull Quelvin's photo from my handbag. "Is this the man who assaulted you?"

I can't help but notice she's shaking.

"Presley?"

"It's *him!*" she whispers.

"That's impossible."

"Why do you keep *saying* that?"

"Because James Quelvin never taught school in Tallahassee."

"He's lying!"

"I just *met* him."

"So?"

"He doesn't match the description you gave Doris or Christine."

She holds up the photo. "This is him, Dani. He's older now, but it's the same guy."

"He can't be."

"Why not?"

"He doesn't have a nose."

Chapter 15

"EXCUSE ME?" PRESLEY SAYS.

"The man I just met, James Quelvin, lost his nose four years ago. You keep saying you got a good look at his face. If that's true, I'm pretty sure one of the first things you would have noticed is he doesn't have a nose."

"He's lying, Dani."

"You can't lie about a *nose*, Presley. Either you've got one or you don't."

"Well he does, and I saw it Sunday night."

"Then how do you explain—"

"You obviously talked to the wrong person. Whoever you spoke to must've been impersonating Mr. Q." She thinks a minute, then says, "Maybe Mr. Q. has a prosthetic nose."

I stare at her for several minutes, trying to decide if she's insane or just crazy. On the other hand, she seems so certain this is the guy, it's hard not to give her the benefit of the doubt.

"Okay," I say.

"Okay what?"

"I believe you."

"You do?"

"I believe what you're saying is possible."

"Thank you."

My phone vibrates. When I pick it up, Dillon says, "I've found Quelvin's alibi."

"Is it solid?"

"I've never seen a better one."

"Let's hear it."

"Sunday evening, at the very time Presley was assaulted, Quelvin was being honored by the Mayor and Chief of Police at the Hadley Hotel, in downtown Gatlinburg."

"Honored for what?"

"Believe it or not, he's a lot like you."

"That statement bears explaining."

"He catches predators."

"Online?"

"Yup. Through his efforts police set up a sting and caught a serial pedophile."

"Cool. Thanks, Dillon."

"My pleasure."

"Can you send me a link to that information?"

"Of course. But I've told you everything there is to read."

"I want to see the photo of the event."

"There wasn't one. At the family's request. And you'll never guess why."

"Can I try?"

"Go ahead. But I guarantee you'll never get it."

"Could it be because he has no nose?"

"You know what you are?" he says. "A fun-sucker! Why didn't you tell me you already interviewed him?"

"I was too interested in what you were saying. What else have you got?"

"Good job!"

"What do you mean?"

"You asked me that in five words!"

"Maybe I'll use just five words for all our exchanges. How about: give it to me straight?"

"I wonder how long this will take to annoy the shit out of me."

"Whatever do you mean, Dillon?"

"Five words again. Yup, question answered. I'm officially annoyed."

"Okay, I'll stop doing that."

"Asshole, you did it again."

"Tell me what you've got."

"Fine. Play your stupid game. Here's something you'll want: the Gatlinburg Quelvin isn't the teacher from Tallahassee."

"You're sure?"

"Only two words this time? Finally! Yeah, I'm sure. I located Quelvin's work records. He's lived in Gatlinburg all his life. Worked at a company called Rainey & Chipping till he quit four years ago and started working for the local police, in their CAC unit."

"What's that stand for?"

"Crimes against Children."

"What happened to the Tallahassee Quelvin?"

"Disappeared."

"What do you mean?"

"No record of him over the past four years."

"Which is around the time Quelvin lost his nose," I say.

"Want me to book flights for you and Presley? The flight ban's been lifted, and Knoxville's only an hour away. You can catch a flight from there to Tallahassee, by way of Atlanta."

"Sounds good. But I'd better check with Sophie first."

"I bet you a week's pay she says no."

"I agree. Which is why I'll invite her to come with us. We can meet up in Atlanta and fly to Tallahassee together."

"Whatever you decide, let me know, and I'll book it."

"Thanks, Dillon."

After ending the call, Presley says, "I think I got most of that. The guy you spoke to claims he works for the police?"

"That's right. He catches pedophiles online."

"In other words, he impersonates a child to attract the attention of perverts."

"That's my understanding."

"So why is it a stretch to think he might be impersonating James Quelvin?"

"Because Dillon has a copy of his work records. He's lived here all his life."

"But I heard you say something about the Tallahassee Quelvin. Does that mean there might be *two* Quelvins?"

"Yes."

"Two *James* Quelvins?"

"According to Dillon, yes. Except that the one who taught you in Tallahassee disappeared in several years ago."

Presley frowns. "You're saying that in the whole United States there's only two Quelvins, and both happen to be named James?"

"Dillon's saying that. Not me."

"And both are approximately the same age?"

"I agree it's a helluva coincidence. So much so that I'd like you to do me a favor."

"What?"

"I want you to go with me to meet the guy you think is impersonating Quelvin."

"Why?"

"I want to rule him out."

"Um...I don't think...I mean, I'm not sure I can face him."

"I'll be there."

"What if the *real* Quelvin's there? The one that attacked me? I know he's got a knife, but what if he has a *gun*? We'd be sitting ducks!"

"You'll drive me there. When I get out, you'll stay in the driveway with the doors locked. I'll lure him onto the front porch so you can get a good look at him."

"And if Quelvin attacks you?"

"You'll dial 911 and drive away as fast as you can."

"I couldn't leave you there with him!"

"He won't do anything if he knows you got away."

"I can't risk it. I'd go crazy if you got hurt trying to help me."

"It's my job. But trust me, he's not going to do anything. He works for the police. I just...I really need you to see this guy so we can be certain he's not the one who taught you in school, or assaulted you at the mall."

She says, "I just identified him from the picture, didn't I?"

"Yes. But like you said, people's appearances change over ten years."

She stares out the window a moment, then turns back to me. "Are you absolutely certain the James Quelvin you spoke to didn't have a nose?"

~Which makes her sound as nutty as I did thirty minutes ago when I asked Quelvin if he was certain he never taught school in Tallahassee.

Chapter 16

"THERE'S A HOUSE FOR SALE TWO DOORS DOWN," Quelvin says. "If you buy it we can chat every day."

"So sorry to bother you again," I say, "but can you do me one last favor?"

"Name it."

"Could you stand on the porch with me and face my car so my friend can see you?"

He sighs. "Is this about my nose?"

"Yes."

"Well, at least you're honest. Is your friend male or female?"

"Female."

"Any chance she might be interested in dating me?"

"None whatsoever."

"You might be *too* honest."

"Sorry."

"Can you at least tell me what this is about?"

"Two nights ago my friend was assaulted in Nashville, Tennessee. She's convinced the man who attacked her is one of her former teachers, from Tallahassee, whom she hasn't seen in ten years. He has a similar name as you, which is how you came to be a possible suspect. I showed her the photo you gave me, and believe it or not, it vaguely resembles her former teacher."

He frowns. "Did you happen to mention I don't have a nose?"

"I did."

"And is she aware I haven't had one for four years?"

"Yes."

"Then how the fuck could I be the guy who assaulted her?"

I say, "Look, I know you didn't do this, but I'd like to convince her, so we can move forward. You'd like that too, wouldn't you?"

"I would. Especially since I fear your friend might be insane."

"Please. She's a sweetheart. Can you humor us just this once?"

He sighs deeply, opens the door, walks to the center of the porch, and turns toward Presley.

And Presley shrieks once, twice—then backs out of the driveway at warp speed. Minutes later, James and I—still shell-shocked on the porch—hear the unmistakable sound of police sirens heading our way.

Lots of police sirens.

Chapter 17

"I CAN'T TELL YOU HOW FRUSTRATING THIS IS," Presley says.

Maybe she can't, but it's frustrating for me, too.

We're sitting in my car, in the parking lot in front of the police station, having spent the past forty minutes in the police station apologizing and explaining. Apologizing: me. Explaining: Presley, who remains convinced James Quelvin raped her two nights ago. The police detectives separated us. I'm not sure what Presley and her detective did, but mine made me provide a complete timeline of Presley's rape, and our subsequent activities.

"This must be a slow day for you guys," I said.

"They're all slow," the detective said. "But I think your client's got serious issues, apart from the rape."

"She's experienced serious emotional trauma. Her husband died in a freak auto accident the same night she was raped. We're talking two days ago, Detective. Her brain's still trying to process it."

"I expect you're right. Still, I have to insist you and your client cease questioning Mr. Quelvin. He doesn't deserve this type of harassment."

"I agree," I said. "Unless he's guilty."

He said, "I can name twenty people who were at the award ceremony for Quelvin Sunday night."

"I'd like to hear the list."

"Starting with my partner and myself, you've got the mayor, the chief of police, the..."

"Names?"

"Excuse me?"

"You said you could *name* twenty people. You're only giving me titles."

"We're not going to let you publicly investigate this man when half the town can vouch for his whereabouts at the exact time of your client's assault. That's harassment."

"I understand."

"Do you? Then why do I get the feeling you believe your client's preposterous claim?"

"Because Presley's *not* a nut job. She might be wrong about Quelvin, but her claim's not spurious. She *believes* what she's saying. I'd bet money she could pass a polygraph."

"Correct me if I'm wrong," he said, "but doesn't that *prove* she's a nut job?" He added, "Quelvin was here Sunday night. I saw him. You can accept that as a fact, can't you?"

"Yes."

His features softened. "I know your story, Dani. You're *The Little Girl Who Got Away*. Must've been hell for you, being abducted and all, and I'm sure you have to relive it every time you get a client with a similar story." He paused. "You've got a sterling reputation with the Nashville PD."

"I *do?*"

"I checked. But you're known for representing fringe clients. I hope you don't let the crazies drag you down."

"Me too."

He looked at me with just enough compassion to feel authentic. "Tell me you know Quelvin didn't do this."

"I know Quelvin didn't do this."

"Thank you."

"You're welcome. Are we free to go?"

"Of course. You could have left at any time. But I'd like to send you off with a parting gift."

"What's that?"

"Two things, really: the first is a warning about the misuse of 911 resources. And the second is a strong recommendation that you help her secure professional counseling, including an immediate psych evaluation."

"Great. And here I was hoping for a toaster."

"Any questions before you go?"

"Just one."

"Shoot."

"Are you absolutely certain James Quelvin doesn't have a prosthetic nose he can attach to his face when in public?"

He sighed. "If he had a prosthetic nose, don't you think he would have worn it Sunday night before accepting his award in front of half the town?"

"Yup."

"Me too. Have a safe trip back to Nashville," he said.

As I walked down the hall toward the front doors, Presley's detective motioned me over and summarized their encounter by saying, "I were you, I'd keep your client away from sharp objects."

Now, in the car, I look at Presley. "You okay?"

"I'm trying to be," she says.

I pull out of the parking lot, turn left on 321 and follow it to Cherokee Road, till I get to the Hadley Hotel.

"What now?" Presley says.

"We're going to talk the manager into letting us look at the security tapes from Sunday night."

"Why would he do that?"

"'Cause we're pretty."

Chapter 18

ROBERT HATMAN ("BITTER BOB," AS WE CALLED HIM LATER), is an equal opportunity letch who's perfectly comfortable staring inappropriately at both of us with equal gusto. I can't say he's strictly a boob guy, but that's where his attention is currently focused, since his desk effectively blocks our lower halves from his unyielding scrutiny. While it creeps me out when *any* guy continues to blatantly check out my "cash and prizes," I'm sure Presley's as thankful as I am that this particular pervert's current view is limited to our cash components. We're sitting across from him on the nastiest cloth chairs I've ever seen in a business that's open to the general public.

How gross are these chairs?

Flesh-eating bacteria gross.

So gross that if Gordon Ramsey walked through the door with his camera crew and semen-detecting black light, hoping to add this filthy fuck trap to his *Hotel Hell* TV series, he'd vomit, burst into tears, and run all the way back to La Tante Claire in Chelsea. The London borough, not Presley's sister-in-law.

"Call me Bob," Robert says, adding, "This oughta be good."

"In what way?" I ask.

"Ya'll want the same thing."

"Who does?"

"Women. You *all* want money."

"We're not like the others," Presley says. "We're different."

"That's what they *all* say. At first." He looks back at me. "*Then* you know what they say?"

"What's that, Bob?"

"They've become accustomed to a certain style of livin', and should be able to *continue* livin' that way."

"You sound recently divorced," I say.

"How'd you guess?"

"I'm intuitive that way."

He shows me a smile that's half-sinister, half-creepy. "You're intuitive, are you?"

"Yup. Amazingly so."

He starts licking his upper lip frantically, like it's on fire, and this is the only way to put it out. "Tell me what I'm thinkin' right *now*, Sugar Pants!" he says. Then, for emphasis—or maybe he's offering a clue—he opens his mouth frightfully wide, and moves his tongue in every possible direction, at lightning speed, like he's a contestant on a game show being forced to remove a piece of tape from his tongue by wiggling it.

"I have a pretty strong idea what you're thinking," I say, "but I'd rather not verbalize it."

He turns to Presley's chest. "How 'bout you?"

"I'm a recent rape victim," she says, without batting an eye.

"You think that bothers *me*?" Bob says.

"I'll guess no," she says.

"And you'd be right." He turns his attention back to my chest. "So the wife tells the judge what a horrible person I am—so horrible she had to cheat on me with my best *friend*! But since she's grown accustomed to havin' a certain lifestyle, I should have to pay her so she can *maintain* it!"

"So you're saying...uh, what, exactly?"

"Two things. First, if I was so fuckin' horrible to live with, why isn't *that* what she's accustomed to? She told the judge I was hateful and abusive. Said I yelled at her all the time and beat her, too. If that's true, and the judge forces me to pay her, he should force me to keep abusin' her, too."

I say, "Let me get this straight: you want to keep *hitting* your ex-wife?"

He winks. "Let's just say I'm *willin'* to, if the judge rules she's entitled to have the same lifestyle at my expense."

I give him the same fake laugh I perfected over the course of a dozen Internet dates back when I thought I might like men if I could just *find the right one*! I'd be sitting across the table from guys old enough to be the fathers of the pictures they posted, trying to be polite to these saliva-dripping, cleavage-staring, Viagra-poppers who fancied themselves charming and witty, but came up shorter than the girl whose feet were visible in her driver's license photo.

"Got it," I say. "What's the second thing? Wait. Was *that* the second thing?" I frown. "Sorry, I'm confused."

"The second thing is, what about what *I've* grown accustomed to?"

"What's that, Bob?"

"You know what I'm talkin' about," he says. He does that tongue thing again. "All I'm sayin', fair's fair. Why can't the judge force her to give me what *I've* grown accustomed to?"

"Why not, indeed?" I say, shamelessly, trying not to throw up in my mouth.

Bob says, "You *get* that, don't you?"

"How could I not? It makes perfect sense: you didn't cheat on her, didn't ask *her* for a divorce. If she wants out and expects to be treated like she was during the marriage, you should have the same right. If you're required to keep paying her after the divorce, she should be forced to keep doing your laundry."

"My *what*?"

"I assume she did your laundry."

"Well...yeah, she did. But—"

"Wouldn't you like your laundry done regularly?"

He smacks his head like he could've had a V-8. "Well...sure! I hadn't thought of that!" He takes a minute to do so, then says, "What about the dishes?"

"She should have to do your dishes, too."

"I like the way you think!" he says.

"Thanks, Bob. You should ask your attorney to draft a proposal: you'll pay her what she wants, but she'll have to come to your place twice a week to do your dishes and laundry, and let you yell at her."

"First few years of marriage she used to give me sex. I grew accustomed to it. I think the judge should force her to keep givin' me sex after the divorce."

"Forcing someone to have sex is called rape, Bob."

"Well, if you're splittin' hairs, maybe."

"I am, and I think the judge will, too."

"What about hittin' her?"

Bob's post-divorce wish list is starting to get longer than the intro to *Game of Thrones*. I say, "I doubt the judge will let you keep hitting her."

He nods. "You're probably right. You think the judge'll grant the other stuff?"

"It only seems fair."

"What about hand jobs? Think he'd approve that on them days she comes over to do my laundry and dishes?"

I wink. "You'll never know if you don't ask."

He grins. "I reckon I have a right to *ask!*"

"It's America, ain't it?" I say, wondering if Presley and I might have passed through a portal to some sort of redneck Narnia when we turned on 321 a while ago.

"If you ain't here for money," he says, "what is it you ladies want?"

"We'd like to take a quick peek at the hotel security tapes from Sunday night's party."

"Party?" he says. "What party?"

For a brief moment I feel like I'm in the middle of a John Locke novel, but then he says, "You mean the *awards banquet?*"

I nod.

"Why would you give a snail's shit about that?"

"We wanted to hear James Quelvin's acceptance speech."

He shakes his head. "That there's one freaky-lookin' motherfucker."

"He was here though? On Sunday night?"

"Sure as hell was."

"You *saw* him?"

"Yup. *Tried* not to stare, but...how do you *not* stare when a mouse fucks a cat?"

"Excuse me?"

"I'm sayin' it ain't natural to see a man with puckered skin where his nose ought to be."

"How long have you known him?"

"Quelvin? All his life, I reckon." He laughs. "We were arrested together."

That gets my attention. "For what?"

He laughs. "Stupid kid shit. Hillbilly hijinks."

"Like what?"

"We broke into an old folks' home one night, locked ourselves in the office, played a song over the loud speaker over and over for two hours straight."

"Why?"

"For the pure meanness of it."

Presley says, "What song?"

"*Daddy There's A Boy Outside.*"

I shrug. "I don't get it." Nor do I care, since I just want to say and do as little as possible, view the security tapes, and get the hell out of Dodge. I feel my phone vibrating, glance at the screen, and see Dillon's trying to call. I reluctantly let it go to voicemail.

Bob says, "Quelvin was pissed his granny sold her house before moving into the old folks' home. It meant him and his mother had to move to an apartment."

"How was it a punishment to play the same song over and over?" Presley asks, while accessing the Internet, despite my frown.

"His granny once said it was the saddest song she ever heard, so he figured to make her cry all night listenin' to it, but after two hours the police came and hauled us to the station."

"They arrested you?"

"Well...not officially. We like to say we were arrested, but they just put us in a cell to scare us. After an hour they called our parents to come get us."

I glance at my phone again and see that instead of leaving a voice mail, Dillon texted:

Call me! Urgent!

Presley says, "The song you're talking about is called *The Men in My Little Girl's Life*."

Bob frowns. "You sure?"

"I'm reading the lyrics right now. It was sung by some guy named Mike Douglas."

He nods. "Yeah, that's the one. There was a *Mike Douglas Show* back then. Old ladies loved him." He chuckles at what I assume is the fond memory of making old ladies cry for two straight hours in a nursing home.

I wait a respectful amount of time, then ask, "How did James lose his nose?"

"No one knows."

"Why not?"

"He won't say."

"This is a small town. Surely *someone* knows."

"Nope. Just James."

"What about the hospital?"

"Nope."

"They would have asked what happened before treating him."

"From what I understand, he never went to the hospital for treatment."

"His family doctor would know."

"James ain't got a family doctor, to my knowledge."

"This is crazy!"

"What's crazy is you needin' to know. Why's it bother you so bad?"

"I don't know, it just does," I say. "Can we see the security tapes?"

He shrugs. "You're a bit...*nosey*, get it?" —I try not to roll my eyes as he adds—"But you're good company. I reckon it'll be all right."

"Thanks, Bob."

Chapter 19

WHILE BITTER BOB BUSIES HIMSELF WITH THE SECURITY CAMERA, I call Dillon, who announces: "Two new wrinkles in the Presley French saga!"

"Tell me."

"Number one is I tracked down the insurance policy."

"How?"

"I hacked into Hailey's Big Iron and pulled Mitch's records."

"Big Iron?"

"That's geek speak for Hailey Memorial Hospital's mainframe computer."

"Why would they have a record of Mitch's life insurance policy?"

"They didn't. But his health insurance was listed, so I hacked into that company's mainframe, and found the policy on the questionnaire he filled out when he applied for his hospitalization insurance. Then I contacted—"

"Dillon? Please: bottom line."

"The policy's in full force, and his sister's the beneficiary."

"*Chelsea* is? You're sure?"

"Yup. Mitch switched from Presley to Chelsea ten weeks ago."

"Is there a loan against the policy?"

"No."

"Hold on." I cover the phone and ask Presley, "Why would Mitch take you off his life insurance policy?"

She frowns. "I guess to punish me for the affair he thought I was having. Did he say Chelsea's the beneficiary?"

I nod.

She shrugs. "It probably wasn't much money."

Back on the phone, I ask Dillon, "How much does Chelsea stand to gain?"

"A hundred grand."

"Presley's right. That's not much."

"It would have paid our fee ten times over," he says.

"I'm sure Presley would rather be safe than have the cash."

When Presley hears that, she says, "I'll be fine, Dani. I think I might be Ron's beneficiary."

"Ron the Pilot?"

She nods.

"What's that worth?"

"Millions, I think."

I stare at her blank expression a minute, and it suddenly occurs to me her phone never pinged. She's had it off since we left my office, and didn't turn it on until looking up

Bitter Bob's song. Mitch has been dead more than 36 hours: long enough for word to get around. Surely *someone* would have called her by now!

But no. Her phone is eerily silent.

I put Dillon on speaker and ask, "What's the second wrinkle in the Presley saga?"

"Mitch's viewing has been set for Thursday, 10 a.m. Funeral's at noon."

"I guess that proves Christine was bluffing about the autopsy. Which funeral home?"

"Pizzleman's. Why? Want me to send flowers?"

"No. I'm trying to figure out how to meet Chelsea alone, so we can have a chat."

"How about her hotel? Fanny and I can start calling around to see where she's registered."

"Okay. Start with the hotels closest to the funeral home and work your way out."

"Will do."

"Wait a sec."

I turn to Presley. Where did Mitch take Chelsea when she came to visit?"

"What do you mean?"

"What's her favorite restaurant?"

"Manny's Italian."

"Dillon, call Manny's Italian to see if Chelsea made a reservation for tomorrow night."

"Why would she do that?"

"It's her and Mitch's favorite restaurant, and the family needs a place to gather before the funeral. They're obviously not planning to use Presley's house or they would have asked her."

"You're good," he says.

Presley asks, "Dillon? Did Mitch get a loan against the policy?"

"No."

"Does that mean I'm safe? It's the only place he could have gotten more than a couple of thousand dollars, and I doubt he could find a hit man for that."

I ask, "Are there any policies on *your* life?"

"No."

"Why not?"

"I'm only twenty-two. I'm in great shape. I don't have a job, so there's no income to replace. Why would we waste money on *that*?"

"I was just thinking Mitch might have agreed to pay the hit man from the proceeds of *your* policy."

"That would make sense if there *was* one. But there's not. Dillon?"

"Yeah?"

"Is Mitch's policy still in force?"

"Yup. Full force, no loans."

"Then Mitch lied about cashing it out to pay the hit man. So I'm safe, right?"

I shake my head. "Not necessarily. If Mitch and Chelsea were as close as you say, she might have paid the hit man out of *her* pocket, and agreed to wait months or years to be repaid from the policy proceeds. Of course, with Mitch dead, she gets the full amount immediately."

Bitter Bob suddenly taps at the door and says, "Got the tapes ready. Sorry there's no popcorn."

I hang up on Dillon so Presley and I can follow Bob into the glorified closet he calls Security Central.

Twenty minutes of time-stamped video and a shitty acceptance speech prove James Quelvin was definitely at the Hadley Hotel in Gatlinburg, Tennessee, on Sunday night, at the exact time Presley claims he was raping her at the Midland Mall in Nashville, 225 miles away.

Oh. And there's this: on the security tapes, he has no nose.

There's only one conclusion to be drawn: James Quelvin could not have been in both cities at the same time, and is therefore even less guilty of raping Presley than I am. He is simply not the man who attacked her. And yet, as I look at Presley watching him on the monitor, I see fear and rage in her face. Her bottom lip is quivering. Tears are flowing freely down her cheeks. I am finally convinced my client is, at the very least, clinically insane. And yes, I know that's not an actual medical diagnosis. But you know what I mean.

I feel so sorry for her.

"It's him!" she says, as sadly as if she just watched the final scene of Toy Story 3. "And he's gonna get away with it."

She puts her head in her hands and cries, softly.

"Here, let me comfort you," Bitter Bob says, moving in for a body hug.

She looks up just in time. "No! ...I mean, thanks for the offer, but...I'm okay."

To me, Presley says, "It's him, Dani. I'd bet my *life* on it."

I sigh. "I know you would, honey."

Chapter 20

ON THE WAY BACK TO NASHVILLE, Dillon has an update for us: "I just saved you fifteen hundred dollars!" he says.

"How so?"

"You no longer have to go to Florida. I found some serious shit on James Quelvin. The one from Tallahassee."

"You located him?"

"Not possible. He really *did* vanish!"

"Who says?"

"The former principal."

"That must've been an interesting conversation."

"You have no idea. Four years ago Tallahassee police came to the school and arrested Quelvin for felony rape of a minor."

"No shit? The case went to trial?"

"Nope. And no one ever heard from him again."

"The police let him *go?*"

"They cited lack of evidence."

"What about the victim?"

"Never named, and the principal refused to say. You want my theory?"

"Dazzle me."

"I think the James Quelvin from Tallahassee was a teacher who'd been in trouble before, in another city. Like Gatlinburg. I think he stole the *real* Quelvin's ID and used it to get a teaching job in Tallahassee."

"Social security numbers wouldn't match."

"He probably changed the number *after* establishing himself in Tallahassee."

"You know his real name?"

"Nope."

"So how do we find him?"

"My opinion? I think we're done. Presley's already turned in the rape kit and filed the police report. I say you talk her into prosecuting the rape case, and let the police do their job. If they send the DNA evidence to CODIS, I bet we get a match."

"Let's hedge our bet."

"How?"

"I like what you said about him being from Gatlinburg. Work your magic."

"Which magic?"

"See if you can find any information about a male teacher being fired from the Gatlinburg school system or surrounding counties between ten and twelve years ago. You'll probably find less than a dozen cases. Then check their addresses to see if they left the area during the six years we know Quelvin was teaching in Tallahassee. The one you can't find is probably our guy."

"How about *you* work the computer and *I* ride around all day with the hot chick?"

"Because hot chicks are your Kryptonite, like computers are mine. Anything else?"

"You remember that FBI impersonator who called you? Agent Peterman?"

"What about him?"

"He's not an impersonator. He's FBI."

"For real?"

"Yup."

I laugh. "What's he want?"

"The reason he called you Monday, the FBI wanted to hire you to see if you could locate five people, including Presley French. Wanna know why?"

"Those five people bought tickets for the flight but didn't show up."

"Right. And the reason he didn't call you back is—"

"They determined it wasn't a terrorist act."

"Right again. Except that now they're convinced it was pilot error. And Ron the Pilot was in command."

"So why's Peterman calling me today?"

"They found out about Presley and Ron's affair, and want to ask her about it."

I shake my head. "And the hits just keep on coming!"

Dillon says, "By the time he's through with her she'll feel responsible for all those lives being lost."

"We'll have to keep her away from him."

"Why would he call the office instead of your cell phone? Everyone in the world's got your cell number."

"He's probably been sitting in our office parking lot all day, hoping to catch Presley before I think to hide her."

"So why call *me*?"

"Peterman's boss probably chewed him out for sitting there all day and getting no results. He probably said to shake some bushes."

"Maybe they've tapped our phone."

"You might be right. Agent Peterman? If you're listening, I'm on my way to Wichita!"

"Kansas?" Dillon says.

"Yup. I've got this Writ of Habeas Corpus that needs to be responded to, and it's a long, hard journey."

"I won't even ask what that's supposed to mean, but if you want to call Agent Peterman, I've got his number."

"Like they used to say on *American Idol*, sorry, it's a no for me."

"What should I tell him when he calls back?"

"Simon Cowell?"

"Agent Peterman."

"Tell him it'll be the coldest day in Kansas history before I say yes."

"Whatever."

Chapter 21

AFTER HANGING UP, I PULL OVER TO THE SIDE OF THE ROAD and tell Presley the FBI knows about her affair with Ron the Pilot. Thing about Presley, you never know how she's going to react. Immediately after being assaulted at Midland Mall she went to the hospital to see Mitch, and never said the first word about being raped. Not to him, or anyone else. And surprisingly, even Mitch failed to sense anything happened to her, or else the nurses would have said something to the police when they called to follow up on Mitch's death. Also, from what I've witnessed, James Quelvin the Rapist doesn't seem to upset her as much as James Quelvin the Noseless.

She says, "If the FBI knows I'm a slut, I guess it's official."

"It gets worse," I say. "The death count from the plane crash has hit 93, and the crash was almost certainly the result of Ron's pilot error."

"I'm not surprised," she says. "Ron has always had a problem with depression."

I give her a look. "Please tell me you didn't break up with Ron just before the flight, hoping he'd take it badly and crash the plane so you could collect the insurance benefit?"

"*Omigod!* What a horrible thought! No! I'm not even positive he *had* insurance, or if he did, that I'm the beneficiary. It's something he said he *wanted* to do, but I never brought it up, and have no idea if he actually did it."

I know you're probably thinking that Presley has little empathy for the crash victims.

Not true.

I know from personal experience she's repressing more emotions right now than Barbara Walters watching Gilda Radner on *Saturday Night Live* reruns. I also know Presley's brain needs time to fully process what's happened, and her healing will have to occur layer by layer, and might require weeks, months, or even years.

We get back to Nashville around eight o'clock, enjoy the dinner Sophie prepared (who knew she could make chicken and dumplings?) Afterward, I take a quick shower and drive to the Landis Inn, where Dillon says Chelsea and her parents are staying. If I can catch her here, I won't have to crash their restaurant get-together tomorrow night.

My plan is to pull an Agent Peterman on her, and call her from the parking lot. I punch her number into my phone, press the call button, and...

"Hello?" she says.

I'm not surprised she accepted my call. Far as she knows I could be anyone who knew her brother, calling to offer condolences.

"Chelsea, my name is Dani Ripper."

"Hi Dani. Were you a friend of my brother's?"

"I never actually met him. But I'm calling because I think you and your husband might be in a bit of trouble."

She pauses. "I'm sorry...who did you say is this?"

"Dani Ripper. I'm a private detective."

"I can see why Presley might hire an *attorney*, but a private *eye*? I'm sorry, but I'm confused. Does she think Mitch is *missing*?"

"She hired me to locate the hit man your brother hired to kill her."

"Uh...*what*?"

"Mitch made a deathbed confession to Presley. Said he hired a hit man to kill her."

"Okay, well it sounds like you've gotten caught up in Presley's insanity. It's simply not true. What you're describing is Presley being Presley. She's paranoid. Thinks men are constantly after her. That bitch will say anything! Except how she cheated on Mitch throughout their entire marriage."

"Eight months," I say.

"What?"

"She cheated on him the last eight months. Not the entire marriage."

"Maybe we should give her a medal for showing restraint those first few months."

"I'm more concerned about the insurance policy your husband wrote on Mitch's life."

"Why?"

"Because Mitch told Presley he cashed it out and used the proceeds to finance a professional hit on Presley French."

"That's preposterous!"

"I agree. But only because we've checked the policy, and it appears to be in full force, with no loans."

"So what's the problem?"

"Two months ago Mitch changed the beneficiary from Presley to you. Any idea why he did that?"

"Yeah. He found out she was cheating on him, and didn't feel she deserved to get the money if something happened to him."

"And something *did* happen."

"It sure as hell did. Her boyfriend killed 93 people, including my brother, Mitch."

"One of the 93 was the boyfriend, though. Look, can we meet for a few minutes?"

"I can't think of a single reason why we should."

"How about this: we've already spoken to the police, and we're about to meet with the FBI."

"About the hit man?"

"That's right."

"How could that possibly affect me and my husband?"

I knew this was coming. Here's the part where I take a risk by stating my assumption as a fact.

If I'm wrong, I'm done. But if I'm right?

Here goes: "Mitch told Presley you knew all about the hit man. The police are going to think you paid the him man out of your pocket, and in return, Mitch named you the primary beneficiary."

"That's bullshit! I had nothing to do with it! The whole thing was a—"

Her voice trails off.

"The whole thing was a what?" I ask.

"Never mind. I don't have to talk to you. I'm about to bury my only brother. I can't believe that bitch is trying to put me through this. She hasn't bothered to contact anyone in the *family*, much less help with the funeral arrangements."

"I've been hiding her. She fears for her life."

"Oh, poo!"

"Poo?"

She sighs. "Do you know where the Landis Inn is located?"

"I do. In fact, I'm in my car, in the Landis parking lot even as we speak."

"Meet me in the restaurant."

"When?"

"Two minutes."

Chapter 22

"THERE'S NO HIT MAN," CHELSEA SAYS. "No one's trying to kill her. The whole thing was a hoax."

"Convince me," I say.

"First of all, you should know your client is a lying, scheming, manipulating, two-faced bitch."

"Wait—don't hold back on *my* account! Personally, I like her. But I'm not here to defend her integrity."

"Good thing, because she has none, far as we're concerned. We *all* hate her, and it's not just the family. Have you met a single friend of hers?"

"No, and no married ones, either. But we've been hiding out, remember?"

"Well, next time you see her, ask how many friends she has. The answer? Zero. She's pond scum. She has no heart, no personality. She's a lump of coal with lipstick. I hate her fucking guts."

"When are you gonna get to the part where you say, 'but I would never hire a hit man to kill her?'"

Chelsea rolls her eyes. "Do I look like the sort of person who'd know the first thing about contacting a hit man?"

"Based on your outfit? No. Makeup? No. Hair style? *Definitely* not! But the anger? Yes, absolutely."

"Well, you're wrong."

"Like I said, convince me. Because if you can't, and *soon*!—our next meeting will be with the FBI."

She takes a deep breath, then spills her guts: "The hit man was a scheme Mitch cooked up months ago for no other reason than to scare Presley. He'd found out about her latest affair, and—"

"Wait. She's had more than one affair?"

Chelsea takes a deep breath. "I...no. Not that I know of. That wasn't fair for me to say. But it wouldn't surprise me. She wasn't a good wife. Anyway, when Mitch found out about the affair I *know* she had, he was devastated. Of course, bitch that she is, she refused to admit the affair, and even went so far as to taunt Mitch about it, saying things like, 'Ron really *intimidates* you, doesn't he!'—you know, trying to needle him. She used to say, 'I can't believe you think I'm having an affair with Ron. He's a friend. We work out together, nothing more. She'd say, 'He's ugly. Have you seen his *teeth*? Trust me, if we got a divorce I wouldn't go running off with *him*!' So Mitch was like, 'Great. She's cheating on me with a guy she doesn't even like enough to *date*!' He was crushed. Talked to me about it all the time, and one day he said, 'It's over. I know she's going to leave me. I wish I could do something to get even with her.'"

"And you said?"

"I told him the best way to punish her was to divorce her first, before she ends it. That would embarrass her publicly and raise his stock in his friends' eyes."

"Was he angry about having to pay her alimony?"

"Furious. But I told him whatever it cost would be worth it, since she'd be more expensive to keep."

"But he didn't agree?"

"He loved her. Kept hoping she'd end the affair, but she never did. Instead, she gave Mitch just enough attention to keep him on the string. No sex, but she'd be pleasant enough to keep him in tow."

"Tell me about the hit man scheme."

"Mitch was locked into that mind frame about punishing her, and wished he knew someone who'd pose as a hit man, to scare the shit out of her and Ron."

"And did he get someone to do that?"

"No, of *course* not! What type of person would agree to do that? We've all watched movies and TV."

I look at her curiously. "I'm not sure what you mean."

"Movie plot: you threaten my husband and his girlfriend, my husband randomly dies, the girlfriend calls the police, your ass goes to jail."

"The people Mitch knows are that forward-thinking?"

"No. I said that to discourage Mitch from what I thought was an awful idea. I don't know Ron, other than he's unstable and brags about carrying a gun. He's been known to lock his ex-wife in the basement when she 'disobeyed' him, and she was glad to stay there, for fear he'd do worse."

"So you thought Ron was a danger to Mitch?"

"I *know* he was. I didn't want anything to happen to Mitch, and I could see a thousand ways this idea could blow up in his face. Mitch finally agreed, and came up with a different version: he said he wouldn't divorce Presley, but but if she wanted a divorce, he'd tell her he cashed out his life insurance policy and used the money to hire a hit man."

"Which brings us back to my original question: did he?"

"No. But he went so far as to ask if I thought my husband, Arthur, would corroborate the story. But I said even if Arthur *did* that—which he wouldn't, since he values his *job*—Presley could simply call the insurance company and they'd tell her the policy was in full force."

"Forgive me for saying this, but Mitch sounds like an angry, petty child."

Chelsea sets her jaw, as if preparing to call me on my comment, but surprises me by saying, "I can understand why you'd say that. But we're talking about the Mitch who was in love with a gorgeous woman who no longer loved him. He was angry. Hurt. Talking about this to me, and me only." She sighs. "And here I am, telling you all about those secret conversations. Presley put him through the ringer, and at the time of those discussions, which took place late at night while his wife was fucking another man—Mitch wanted her to suffer because she'd made him suffer. He didn't want to hurt her, just scare her. In his mind, at the time, what better way to punish her than make her and her boyfriend fear for their lives?"

"I can think of one: how about actually killing her?"

"Maybe he *would* have, if he had the contacts or the guts. But he didn't, and he just kept...*living* with her, hoping she'd stop fucking around, right under his nose....Excuse me, but are you *smiling* right now?"

—If I am, it's because of the nose reference, though I'd prefer not to explain that to Chelsea, since she might wonder what kind of person would find humor in meeting a man with no nose. So I say, "My face just looks like I'm smiling sometimes."

"Well it doesn't look like it now."

I change the subject: "You still haven't given me a credible reason to doubt Mitch's deathbed confession."

"The *timing's* the best proof," she says. "He talked about it for months, and the trigger event was going to be the day she asked him for a divorce. But she never did, so he never played the trick. Then, suddenly, he found himself in the hospital on the night she was supposed to be on the plane with Ron, flying to Atlanta for a fun-filled weekend of illicit sex. But Mitch had a seizure, and a death premonition. The timing was perfect. I didn't know he was going to do it, but I'm sort of glad he did, because it obviously worked. He obviously frightened her, and that means he died with some measure of satisfaction and dignity."

"Did he tell any of his friends about the hit man scheme?"

"I doubt it. His friends have wives, and he wouldn't have wanted everyone talking about it, making fun of him."

"But he felt safe talking to you about it?"

"Of course. I knew he was hurt, and needed to vent. And of course he had one huge problem that kept him from going through with the scheme."

"What's that?"

"Making the threat sound believable. For Mitch, the worst thing would be if Presley laughed in his face. Plus he knew if she called the insurance company, they'd tell her the policy was in full force. So he made me his beneficiary."

"How did that help?"

"First, it was a slap in Presley's face. She'd find out about it during the divorce, or after his death. Second, he knew the insurance company would refuse to give her details about the policy if she called them."

"Why's that?"

"She would no longer have an insurable interest."

"So you're saying when Mitch wound up in the hospital, and realized he could die, he finally saw an opportunity to use the phony hit man story to scare Presley?"

"That *has* to be what happened. Because I thought he was done with the whole idea. He hadn't mentioned it for weeks."

"Why were you willing to talk to *me* about it?"

"I don't want my husband to lose his job."

"Why would that happen?"

"Arthur wrote the policy, I'm the beneficiary. If the police and FBI launch some sort of investigation, who knows what might happen? I don't want Mitch's stupid idea to wind up getting Arthur fired, or give them a reason to deny the death benefit."

I study her face very carefully as I ask, "What about the rape?"

"What rape?"

"Mitch told Presley the hit man offered him a discount to rape Presley before killing her."

She closes her eyes, shakes her head. "Are you being serious with me right now? Because that's a whole new wrinkle, and a stupid one, at that. But it does sound like Mitch, going too far, trying to squeeze out the last drop of anger."

"Except that Presley was raped Sunday night, before visiting Mitch in the hospital."

She coughs out a bitter laugh. "That's total bullshit! And so typical of Presley to say. Please tell me you don't believe her!"

"Sorry to disappoint you, but I *do* believe her. Maybe it's because I personally took her to the rape exam and helped her file the police report."

"There was proof?"

Both physical trauma and DNA evidence."

"Well, if you're only talking about cuts, bruises, and sperm, you'll probably find it's the result of rough sex with her boyfriend, earlier in the day."

"She was raped in a fucking parking lot, Chelsea!"

"Her story."

I take a deep breath. Then say, "You've made it abundantly clear you hate Presley, and I'm sure the feeling's mutual. But as a woman, I'm appalled and quite disappointed in your attitude."

"If I were you I'd feel the same way. But your client is a pathological liar."

"Whether she is or isn't, she was definitely raped, and Mitch warned her it was coming. Can you see why the police will want to question you and Arthur?"

"Arthur knows nothing about this."

"How much do *you* know?"

"Only what I've told you. There *is* no hit man."

"Would you be willing to take a polygraph?"

"Yes. I'll take one right now if you can arrange it."

"How about tomorrow morning, at my office?"

"What time?"

"Nine o'clock work for you?"

"Give me the address."

I do. Then, clearly annoyed, she asks, "How long is this going to take?"

"An hour, give or take. Why, is there someplace you need to be?"

"Did you really just ask me that? My brother *died*! People are arriving from out of town. His viewing is—" she checks her watch "—less than thirty-six hours from now. We're burying him two hours after that, and we haven't even picked out a *cemetery* plot yet!"

"Right. Sorry, I completely lost track of...uh...Never mind. I'm sorry."

"And *you're* disappointed in *my* attitude? Jeez *Louise*!" she says.

Really? Jeez Louise?

I *hate* that expression! It's so stupid! Look, I know Jeez is a way to keep from saying Jesus, but who the fuck's Louise? Just some stupid name that rhymes with Jeez? Why not say Jeez Please, or Cheese, or Jeez Trapeze?

But I deserve her attitude. I was so convinced she hired the hit man, and so stunned to hear she's willing to take a polygraph to prove she didn't—I temporarily forgot why she came to town in the first place. I apologize again, and slink to my car.

At first, I just sit here, bashing myself for being so insensitive. Then I see her staring at me through the restaurant window, which causes me to shrink down in my seat and slide toward the floor, while wishing there was someplace I could go where she'd never be able to see or find me...

And then it hits me: I know exactly what happened to Quelvin, and where he is.

Chapter 23

"WITSEC!" I SAY, BREATHLESSLY.

"Exactly!" Dillon says. "But...how did you *know*? I was just about to call you and tell you the same thing! Where *are* you?"

"In the parking lot of Chelsea's hotel."

"Have you found her yet?"

"Just spoke to her. She said the same thing you did: Presley's safe. According to her, the whole thing was a big hoax. Mitch kept the idea in his back pocket for months, and decided to scare the shit out of Presley when she'd believe him most."

"Deathbed confession. You believe her?"

"Yeah."

"Wait. You *do*? You never believe *anyone!*"

"I'll believe her more after her polygraph."

"You're serious? She agreed to a polygraph?"

"She's coming to our place at nine tomorrow morning."

"That's not enough notice."

"Call Fanny. She made it happen last time with little notice. Tell her it's an emergency."

"I'll try."

"Don't try. Do."

"Yes, Yoda." He pauses. "So how'd you figure out the Tallahassee Quelvin was in Witness Protection?"

"I kept wondering how a guy could be charged with raping a minor, then get the case thrown out for lack of evidence, and then disappear. So that was in the back of my mind. Then, a few minutes ago, I said something stupid to Chelsea that embarrassed me so badly I wanted to crawl into a hole somewhere and hide, but there was no place to go, since I was in plain sight. Which made me wonder if there's any way a person could hide in plain sight, and I could think of just one: Witness Protection."

"So it was a hunch?"

"Let's call it deductive reasoning. How did *you* arrive at the same conclusion?"

"I tracked the incidents of male teachers who were fired for inappropriate conduct involving students in the nine counties surrounding Gatlinburg during the years we know Quelvin was in Tallahassee."

"And?"

"Only one had disappeared."

"But that could mean he died."

"True. But there was no death certificate."

"He could have been kidnapped, killed, and buried in the woods somewhere."

"Always a possibility, but wouldn't you expect someone to file a missing person report?"

"I would. What else tipped you off he might be in WITSEC?"

"He was rumored to have mob connections."

"Ah! Nicely done! What's his name?"

"Adam Elliott."

I frown. "That can't be right."

"Why not?"

"Does the name Adam Elliott sound like a serial rapist to you?"

"Not really."

"And it sounds even less like a guy with mob connections."

"Maybe he was born with a proper criminal-sounding name, but changed it to Adam Elliott when he entered WITSEC the first time."

I think about it. "You might have something there. Maybe he was already in WITSEC before he got in trouble in the Tennessee school system. Maybe the US Marshall's Service relocated him to Tallahassee, and gave him the name James Quelvin."

Dillon says, "Actually, WITSEC lets the participants change their own names. They recommend you keep the same initials, and same first name, but you don't have to."

"You can choose any name you want?"

"Yup."

"Elliott probably knew James Quelvin, or had heard of him, and liked the name."

"More likely, he wanted a name with a history. Then he forged a teaching certificate, taught school a few years, moved to Tallahassee, raped a kid...got reassigned, and changed his name again."

"It would explain how he wound up with Quelvin's name," I say, "and how he managed to disappear into thin air twice."

"I feel really good about this, Dani!"

"I wish I shared your enthusiasm."

"Why don't you?"

"Because...how the hell are we going to find him if he's in Witness Protection?"

Dillon says, "Would Donovan Creed have access to those types of records?"

"Certainly not *legal* access, but..."

"Maybe you should call him."

I sigh. "I should probably call him sometime when I *don't* need something."

"He loves you. He'll do anything for you."

"You think?"

"Call him."

"I'll think about it. Maybe I'll call him tomorrow morning, before Chelsea's polygraph."

Chapter 24

FOR THE FIRST TIME SINCE I'VE KNOWN HIM, Creed doesn't take my phone call. Instead, he texts:

I've gone dark. I'll call when I can.

Shit. I really want to ask if he can breach WITSEC, but he won't call back till he's finished doing whatever he's doing, which means I'll have to wait, and you know how I hate to wait! Especially when I don't know how *long* I'll have to wait.

Presley's hanging with Sofe. In less than an hour, Chelsea will be here for her polygraph, and we'll know if the threat to kill Presley is real.

I'm bored.

According to the clock on the wall, Chelsea's arrival is fifty minutes away.

What to do?

I buzz Fanny, who answers in her annoying Bugs Bunny voice: "Eh...What's up, Boss?"

"Any clients I need to call?"

"*Clients?* What does *that* mean? Hey Dillon! Can you explain the meaning of this?"

"What?" I hear him say in the background.

She says, "Dani wants to know if she can call any of our hundreds of clients."

"Please inform my partner we have no clients at all," Dillon says, "and therefore none to call. Other than Presley French, of course. Tell her Agent Peterman, from the FBI, is still waiting to hear from her."

Fanny gives me Peterman's number. I write it down on my scratch pad, stare at it a minute, then call James Quelvin, from Gatlinburg. When he answers, I say, "Hi James, it's me, Dani."

"Don't tell me you're still in town?"

"Nope. You're safe. I'm back in Nashville."

"What do you want?"

"I was wondering how you lost your nose."

"Why do *you* care?"

"I can understand if you don't want to talk about it."

"Good. Because I don't."

"Is that your biggest secret?"

"Excuse me?"

"If I tell you my biggest secret, will you tell me how you lost your nose?"

"No."

"Why not?"

"Because I don't give a shit about your secrets."

"Well *that's* rude!"

"Sue me. You know what *else* is rude? Harassment."

"I'm just asking a simple, polite question. Like if you asked me if I had a boob job."

"Did you?"

"No."

"Well maybe you should. They're pretty small."

"Let's try to stay on the subject of how you lost your nose."

"Why do you care?"

"I hate not knowing things."

"Surely there are other mysteries you can focus on. You can't know everything else in the world."

"Sorry, you're wrong. I know everything else in the world except what happened to your nose. When I learn that, there'll be nothing left to know."

"Well, you'll just have to find a way to live without that knowledge."

"You can't *do* this to me! It's making me crazy! It's like an itch I can't reach."

"Sorry."

"C'mon, James. Don't you want to hear my biggest secret? It's really good! Probably the best secret you'll ever hear."

"Sorry. Not interested."

"Let me give you all my phone numbers, in case you change your mind."

"That won't be necessary."

"James?"

"Yeah?"

"Take down my fucking numbers."

He sighs, I give him my numbers, then hang up. Then I call Agent Peterman, who starts off our conversation saying, "I don't like you."

"Why not?" I say.

"For one thing, you're unprofessional. For another—"

"Fuck you!" I shout, and hang up.

Dillon buzzes me. "What's *wrong* with you?"

"I don't know how Quelvin lost his nose."

"You cussed out an FBI agent because of Quelvin's nose?"

"I can't help it. It's making me crazy."

"Why?"

"I can think of hundreds of ways it could have happened. Last night I couldn't sleep, so I stayed up half the night counting nostrils."

"You're insane."

"Help me, Dillon. Work your magic. Find the answer."

"We've got a polygraph coming up."

"Yeah. In forty-two minutes."

"Is the man's nose really that important?"

"No. But his *lack* of a nose is."

"I'll see what I can do."

Fanny buzzes. "Archie's here."

"Who's that?"

"Polygraph guy."

"It's early," I say.

"I'll put him in the conference room, but we need to talk."

"You and him?"

"You and me."

"Okay."

By the time Fanny gets the polygraph guy situated in the conference room, Dillon's in my office saying, "There's no Internet information on James Quelvin beyond what I've already given you, and nothing about his nose."

"That blows," I say.

"Snaps for worst pun ever," he says.

"Speaking of blows," Fanny says, entering my office, "No big deal, but I promised Archie a blowjob."

Dillon's ears turn red. "Why would you offer *that*?"

She smiles, flicks her cleaved tongue. "You're so *cute* when you're jealous."

"I'm *not* jealous," he pouts. "I just don't understand why you'd have to offer him... *sex* to do what he's *paid* to do."

"It was the only way to get him here without notice. He was booked all morning with the FBI doing polygraphs on some Columbians."

"Why?"

"How should *I* know? Maybe they're trying to find out why South America stole our name."

"What about Central America?" Dillon says.

"Probably have *them* scheduled for tomorrow. Regardless, Archie was booked all day. Then *you* called last night and said, 'Fanny, get him here! I don't care what it takes!' Did you not say that?"

"I did."

"Well, that's what it took. Double pay, and a blow job."

"That's totally unprofessional!" I say, "and I worry what it could lead to if word gets out: plumbers, repairmen, mail carriers—all refusing to do their jobs unless they get blown..." I sigh. "But since you promised, I suppose you'd better hurry up and get it over with, before Chelsea shows."

"Not so fast," Fanny says. "What about Beth Conroy, your little school teacher girlfriend?"

"What about her?" I say, defensively.

"Another instance of you needing a polygraph guy with no notice, and me being forced into taking one for the team."

"Along with a hefty bonus, as I recall."

"Nevertheless, on that fateful day I did my duty with Mike the polygraph guy. Unfortunately, I performed *too* well, as evidenced by the permanent arrhythmia he sustained."

"You never told me you *blew* him!" Dillon says, angrily.

"Dear boy. You, of all people should know how skilled the International Order of Virgin Boat Festival Princesses are, when it comes to mouth work."

"You never said you *blew* him," Dillon repeats.

"Don't pout, Dillon," I say. "It's bad for your frown lines. Fanny? I sense you're trying to make a point. What is it?"

"Polygraph operators are a small group, and word gets around, so Archie—having heard about Mike's experience—refused my offer. Said he wouldn't come unless..."

"Unless what?" I say.

"I told him *you'd* blow him."

"*What?*"

Dillon bursts out laughing. "What's the matter Dani?"

"Unacceptable!" I say.

Dillon says, "What was it you just said to Fanny? 'I suppose you'd better hurry up and get it over with, before Chelsea shows up?' Sounds like good advice!" He laughs some more.

Fanny says, "Don't wear yourself out laughing, Boy Wonder. Archie said no to Dani. He wanted *you*. So..."

Dillon's face turns crimson.

My turn to laugh.

He looks at Fanny. "Like Dani said, that's totally unacceptable."

"Oh really? Then why was it acceptable a minute ago, when you thought *I* was gonna do it?"

Dillon and I look at each other. I say, "I'm sorry, Fanny. I think we just assumed you enjoyed doing that to strange guys."

She says, "Well, I do. But I don't like being taken for granted. More than anything, I just want to be accepted here."

"It might help if you showed up for work more than twelve times a year."

Dillon says, "Let's not go down that road. What about Archie?"

Fanny says, "If he doesn't get what he came for, he's gonna walk."

"What if we offer him more money?"

"We're already paying him double."

"Offer another hundred," I say.

She rolls her eyes and says, "Dillon? How much would someone have to pay *you* to blow a guy?"

"A billion dollars."

"And to receive one?"

"From a guy?"

She nods.

"A million dollars."

"Be honest."

"A hundred grand. But we're not paying him a hundred grand for a polygraph," Dillon says.

"You're not paying him a hundred dollars, either," Fanny says.

"Five hundred?" I say.

She thinks a moment. "That might do it. But make the check out to me."

"Why?"

"Because I'm taking tomorrow off to go on a spa day, and that's how much I plan to spend."

"I thought you said Archie wasn't interested because of what happened to the last guy."

"True. But when I'm alone with him in the conference room, and tell him I'm the only game in town...what's he gonna say?"

"I don't know."

"Try again."

"Thank you?"

She smiles. "You're welcome."

Chapter 25

"UNCLE SAL'S GOT NOTHING," SOPHIE SAYS.

"No word of a hit on Presley?" I ask.

"Nope. And if anyone in this part of the country took the contract, he'd know."

"Just to clarify, Sal's saying no offer's been made, no permission's been given, and there's no word on the street."

"Word on the *street?*" Sophie says, laughing. "Where'd you hear that?"

"I watch TV. Did he ask his associates?"

"Yes."

"Other crime bosses?"

"He didn't say, but I'm sure he did. What happened with Chelsea: did she take the polygraph?"

"She did."

"And?"

"She passed with—as they say on TV—flying colors, though I have no idea why they say that. I mean, colors can't fly, and even if they could, why would *flying* colors be considered better than stationary ones when it comes to polygraph tests? I mean, why are colors even mentioned in the first—"

She cuts me off: "I'll put Presley on the phone."

She does, and I give Presley the good news, and finish my rant about flying colors, and she asks, "Does this mean there's no hit man?"

"That's exactly what it means. The whole thing was a hoax."

"You're sure?"

"Positive. Our contacts have no knowledge of a hit, and Chelsea passed the polygraph."

"There's no way she could be lying?"

"Our polygraph guy was thorough. He asked if Mitch hired someone to kill you, and she said no, and that was the truth. He asked if Mitch discussed trying to scare you by pretending to hire a hit man. She said yes, and *that* was the truth. He asked if she had any knowledge a hit man had been *contacted* to kill you and she said no, and that was the truth. He asked if she ever had a conversation with an actual hit man or spoke to someone else about getting a hit man. She said no, and that was the truth. He asked about the insurance policy, and she repeated everything she told me last night, and that was the truth. He asked if you were in any danger from any possible threat she was aware of. She said no, and that was the truth."

"Wow! Fantastic! Thanks!"

"You're welcome. I'm very pleased about this, though I could strangle your husband for putting you through it."

"If you're serious, I know where his body will be from ten to noon tomorrow morning!"

"Wouldn't *that* be something for the guests to talk about!"

We laugh till Presley says, "Does this mean I can finally go home?"

I stop laughing. Did she just say *finally*? "Uh...yeah, sure, Presley. Go ahead. I had no idea you were so *miserable* at our place."

"Don't be silly! You and Sofe have been great. You've treated me like royalty. I just meant—"

"*Sofe?*"

"Huh?"

"Did you just call my girlfriend *Sofe?*"

"Yes, of course. You were right there when she asked me to."

"That's what *I* call her."

"Oh. Okay, well...sorry, I...uh...didn't realize it was...a pet name, or whatever."

"*Pet?* You think of Sophie as my *pet?*"

"*What?* Of *course* not! What I meant was..." she thinks a minute. Then giggles. "You're punking me, aren't you!"

"Huh?"

"You're imitating the scene from *Goodfellas!*"

I have no idea what she's talking about, but if she thinks I'm acting crazy, she's right.

I am.

I shake my head. What the fuck's wrong with me? The girl just wants to go home, get back to her life, have some privacy; wear her own clothes. Of *course* Sofe told her to call

Don't Tell Presley!

her Sofe. *All* our close friends call her that. It doesn't *mean* anything. What's my *problem*?

Is it Quelvin's nose?

No.

I mean, yeah, that's bothering me, but the truth is, I'm angry and frustrated with Presley because of something Chelsea said after showing up for her polygraph. She said: "I've been thinking all night about Presley being raped. If she really *was*, I feel terrible for the things I said."

"She was definitely raped," I said, solemnly.

Chelsea said, "Then again, I'm really sorry. I'm not a fan of hers, but no one deserves that."

"Nice of you to say. For the record, why'd you assume Presley was lying? Has she ever claimed to be raped before?"

"Not that I know of. I think I just assumed it was another one of her bullshit James Quelvin stories."

While I was busy thinking *WTF?* Chelsea said, "Presley routinely claims she sees her old junior high teacher following her around, intending to rape her."

So there's that. Also...wait. Somewhere in the background I hear Presley on the phone saying, "Dani? It's *Goodfellas*, right?"

I'm also upset Creed didn't take my call. It concerns me I might have imposed one time too many on our friendship. I really should have called him sometime, just to chat, when I didn't *need* something from him. I think about it all the time, but always back off, worrying about interrupting his personal time. I also tell myself if he wanted to talk to me, he'd call. Then again, maybe he's overthinking our friendship the same way I am. Maybe he feels *he'd* be imposing if he called. Nevertheless, I'm dying to know if the Tallahassee Quelvin's in WITSEC, and if so, did he relocate to Nashville? I might be naïve, but despite what Chelsea said, and despite her misidentifying the nose-less Quelvin, I still find myself clinging to a slender thread of belief in Presley, and want to believe the Tallahassee Quelvin raped Presley Sunday night. If so, I want him in prison and off the streets, and at the moment Creed's my only hope to make that happen.

So this is the gumbo of frustration that's responsible for my sudden nastiness toward Presley. She's still on the phone, trying to figure out why I'm being so mean. Okay, this is going to be awkward as hell, but here goes: I suck it up and say, "Presley, you nailed it! That was my attempt at recreating the *Goodfellas* scene."

She pauses a moment, then channels her inner Joe Pesci, and snarls, "You think that's *funny*? Funny *how*? I mean, funny like I'm a *clown*? I *amuse* you? I make you *laugh*?"

I *do* laugh. "You're way better at it than me. I'm going to miss you."

"What about my case?"

"I'm still working on it. Like I said, we think the Tallahassee Quelvin might be in Witness Protection. I'm waiting to hear from someone who might be able to help us."

"Donovan Creed?"

"Yeah, but you should probably forget you ever heard that name."

"Why?"

"He's got enemies in high places."

"Aren't you concerned for *your* safety?"

"Not so much. It's fairly well known I'm his friend. People tend to leave Creed's friends alone."

"So...where does that leave us?"

"I think we're done, for the time being. You've got a lot on your plate, a lot of issues to deal with. You'll need to go through Mitch's personal effects, records, figure out your finances, and so forth, and you'll probably want to call Ron's family and find out if you are, in fact, on any of his life insurance policies."

"*That* would be weird."

"You're right. I'll have Dillon make that call. Also, if you need anything, I'm just a phone call away. If it's something I can't do personally, I can find someone who can. I'm not abandoning you, Presley, just giving you however much space you need. But if there's anything I can do—"

"Would you consider following me home? I'm kind of nervous about going there alone. This whole situation's gonna be difficult. I've never been alone before."

"I understand. I'm glad to do it. I'll even stay a while and help you get settled in."

"*Really?* You're the best! Um...can you bring your gun, just in case?"

I laugh. "You don't want that. I'm not very good with my gun in stressful situations. Ask Fanny, if you need corroboration! I shot at her in the office once, by accident, and... well, it's not important. But truly, there's nothing to worry about. I'm convinced the hit man was a hoax. My only question is when do you want to go?"

"Well, I've already showered, and there's nothing to pack, so I'm ready whenever it's convenient for you. No rush, just whatever fits your schedule."

"As luck would have it, I'm available right now."

When we get to Presley's, we check the closets, under the beds, behind the curtains, every square inch of the attic and basement...

No hit men.

I sit with her an hour while she cries over her dire circumstances: she's alone, unemployed, overwhelmed, and has no idea where to go from here. When she's thoroughly cried out, I tell her to change the locks in case Mitch's sister or parents have a set of keys. I also give her three portable locking devices to better secure the doors. After demonstrating how they work, I hug her and say, "We'll keep working the case, and the minute I have something for you, I'll call. And same goes for you: if anything changes, or you think of anything that might help us find the real Quelvin, or if you need help navigating the next few days or weeks, or just want someone to talk to—"

"Thanks, Dani. I'll call. But...if I haven't heard from you by Monday, can I come over and watch *The Bachelor* finale with you guys?"

I smile. "That would be...*amazing!*"

I hug her again, and leave.

Four hours later, she's on the phone, breathlessly telling me she just saw James Quelvin.

The real one, from Tallahassee.

Chapter 26

"ARE YOU SURE IT WAS QUELVIN?" I ASK.

"Positive!" she whispers.

"Where *are* you?"

"Airport."

"*Why?*"

"My mother flew in to be with me."

"I'm confused. When was this arranged?"

"It wasn't arranged, and honestly, I don't want her here. But her plane's about to land, so what can I do?"

"I'm sure she just wants to comfort you."

"She thinks I'm crazy. I have no idea how she found out about Mitch, 'cause *I* certainly never told her! Anyway, she got on a plane this morning without telling me, called from Atlanta, and demanded I pick her up."

"You never told your mom that Mitch died?"

"Nope."

"Why not?"

"*This* is why! You think I want her *here? Staying* with me?"

—My thought on that is, of course! If my husband died I'd absolutely want my mom beside me, comforting me. But I'm not Presley, and know nothing about her mommy issues, so I say, "Tell me about seeing Quelvin."

"Have you ever been someplace you thought was safe, but suddenly had a creepy, cold feeling?"

"Sure. Every day, in my office. But it's just Fanny."

"I was standing in the gift shop, and suddenly had that kind of feeling. I turned around just in time to see Quelvin walking down the hallway."

"Was he a *passenger*? Had he just arrived from somewhere?"

"I think he was boarding a flight, 'cause he was rolling a bag behind him. But he could also be an airport employee."

"What makes you say that?"

"There was a guy sweeping. A porter. I'm pretty sure Quelvin spoke to him."

"Did he stop and talk, or was it more like nodding as he walked by?"

"More like nodding."

"Why are you whispering?"

"I'm still in the gift shop, and there are people all around me."

"Where's Quelvin now?"

"I don't know. He kept walking."

"I don't suppose you can try to follow him, maybe get a photo?"

"I already got his photo."

"What?"

"I snapped it as he walked by. You want me to text it to you?"

"Yes, of course!"

"Okay, here goes."

While I wait for the photo to show up, Presley says, "My mom can't know any of this, okay?"

"Which part?"

"*All* of it."

"Why not?"

"Like I said, she already thinks I'm crazy. If she hears about the...rape and stuff, she'll try to have me committed. Did the picture come through?"

"Yes and no."

"What do you mean?"

"I got a photo, but not the one you meant to send."

"What do you mean?"

"Look at it."

"I just did. What's wrong?"

"It looks nothing like him."

"I told you he's ten years older than the picture we saw yesterday. But surely you can see the resemblance."

"Sorry."

"Dani? You sound funny. Are you okay?"

"I'm fine. Are *you* okay?"

"I'm a little shaken up, but yeah, I'm all right."

"And you think this photo I'm staring at, the one you just texted me...is James Quelvin, the man who raped you? Is that what you're saying?"

"You sound like you don't believe me!"

"It's not that, it's just—"

"It's him, Dani. It's Quelvin. My school teacher. I'm 100% positive."

I stare at the picture again. "Can I just come right out and say it?"

"Please do."

"The man in this picture is black."

"What do you mean?"

"He's African American."

"It's Quelvin, Dani. I know he appears different to you in that picture, but it's him. And he either works here, or he's getting ready to board a flight. We can't let him get away!"

I sigh. "Okay. I'm on my way."

"I won't be here, 'cause of my mom. I don't want her to know about this."

"So you've said. Okay, I'll check it out."

"How?"

"I'll buy a ticket to somewhere, go through security, and check each gate. If he's not there, I'll find the guy who was sweeping, and show him the picture. At least we'll know if he works at the airport."

"You don't sound very optimistic."

"I'm sorry. I'm just struggling with this."

"Well, do your best," she says, cheerfully.

Cheerfully?

After we end the call I stare at my phone and wonder why, out of all the private investigators in Nashville, I'm the one who gets the nutjobs? I start every case with the optimism of a mail order bride, but more often than not I get the feeling my clients have lured me into a strange place on an improbable pretext, and I find myself in a total fog, as if I'm in the middle of a dream, and the room around me is swirling, and I just want it to stop. So I reach around with my hands to see if I can find something—*anything!*—that will ground me, but all I come up with is a pair of panties, and wonder if they're mine, and if so, am I going to wake up to the sound of Bill Cosby's voice, calling for a cab?

Chapter 27

"EXCUSE ME, SIR?"

"Wow!"

"Can I speak to you a minute?"

"You can speak to me every day for the rest of my life!"

I show him Presley's photo. "Have you seen this woman?"

His eyes light up. "I sure have! That there's a once-in-a-lifetime beauty."

I frown. "You think?"

He says, "You see a woman looks like that, you never forget it."

"Fine. You *saw* her. Now—"

"I remember the day, the time, the place, the song playin' on the music tape in the background, the—"

"Let's move along, okay?"

He shrugs.

I take out my phone, press the record button. "What's your name?"

"Stay Busy the Porter."

"Your *real* name."

"That'll work."

I frown. "What should I call you?"

"Honey."

"Mr. Busy, this isn't the type of interview where you're going to charm me with your personality. I'm investigating a rape, and quite honestly, I think you might know the perpetrator."

"Why, 'cause I'm *black*?"

"Yes."

"*Excuse* me?"

"Uh...I mean, no. Not *just* because of that. But the victim identified her assailant as a black man, and she was here at the airport fifteen minutes before the assault took place."

"So why you askin' *me*? There are other men of color workin' here."

"True. But you were seen talking to him."

"Was *Weevil* seen talkin' to him?"

"I don't know what that means."

"I seen you talkin' to Weevil just now. Before you come to me. Did he talk to the black man in the picture too?"

"I don't know any Weevil. The only person I've spoken to is Jubal, the shoe shine guy."

"That's Weevil. And I can't help but notice he's black, too."

"Oh really? What tipped you off?"

"The color of his skin."

"That's racist," I say.

"Girl, you ain't got a clue about what's racist."

"Why do you call him Weevil?"

"'Cause his shoe polish is made from beetle shit."

"That can't be true."

"Well, not the whole can, but the shellac part is. It's the same ingredient you'll find on jelly beans."

"Now I *know that's* not true!"

"Well, it's easy enough to prove. You got a fancy phone in your hand. Press them buttons and look it up on the Internet. You'll find it's beetle shit that gives the jelly bean its shine. I bet you'll be tellin' all your fancy friends about it tonight."

"I love the Internet," I say. "You can look up anything, they've got the answer. I looked up 'why do guys always shout when advertising furniture and race car events on TV,' and within seconds got the answer: turns out they're possessed by shape-shifting vampires! Who knew?"

"I ain't sure I believe *that*," he says. "But jelly beans and Weevil's shoe polish—them things have beetle shit in 'em."

"Well, Mr. Weevil—I mean Jubal—never mentioned that fact."

"You didn't ask him?"

"No, and he didn't tell me."

"That strike you as odd?" he says, with a sly grin.

"What's that?"

"You show him a picture of a rapist and he don't think to tell you his polish has beetle shit in it?"

"No. And I think you're messing with me."

"Oh really? What tipped you off?"

We laugh, 'cause that's what I said to him a minute ago. Then I ask, "Is it true about the jelly beans?"

"It is."

"I'm still gonna look it up."

"You do that." He points down the hall. "They sell stale ones in that gift shop right there, case you want to trick your friends."

"Don't think I won't! I'm gonna carry jelly beans around from now on. I won't tell people they're made out of beetle shit till after they eat some."

"I hope you plan to pay me a royalty for all that fun you're gonna have with that information I gave you."

"Nope. Sorry."

"Spoken like a true woman."

"That's sexist."

"Uh huh. Everything's somethin' with *you* people, ain't it?"

"*Excuse* me? Did you just say *you* people?"

"I sure did. Is that racist, or sexist?"

"I'm not sure," I say. "But we should probably go ahead and get down to business."

"Okay. Lay it on me, sweet thing."

I show him my phone and tap the screen to enlarge the photo.

He frowns. "You think that looks like me?"

"No, and I never said it did. This is the man I'm trying to find. Like I said, you were seen talking to him."

"Well, he looks sort of familiar, but I'm not sure I can recognize him for certain without thinkin' on it a spell. But you know what I *can* recognize?"

"What's that?"

"A twenty dollar bill."

I frown. "A twenty, huh?"

"Oh, yes, indeed. Nothin' looks like a twenty, or smells like one, neither."

"You think you can smell the difference between a twenty and other denominations?"

"You best *believe* I can! Hell, lady, I can sniff the *green* off a twenty."

I reach into my jeans pocket, pull out a twenty, hand it to him. "Will *this* help your memory?"

He stuffs it in his pocket. "It already has! I can *definitely* tell you I never seen this passenger before. And if we spoke, it was just to say hi."

"If you don't *know* him, why'd you identify him as a passenger? I never said he was."

"Didn't need to." He points at the photo. "See that little white square in his hand? That's his baggage claim ticket." He cocks his head to get a better look at my face. "Why, you're beautiful!" he says. "You could almost be her twin sister!"

I say, "Why, because we all look alike?"

He chuckles. "Only in my sweetest dreams, young lady." He turns, starts walking away.

I call out: "Wait! Mr. Busy? One last question?"

He stops and turns. I walk closer and say, "The evening you saw her."

"What about it?"

"Where was she?"

"Gate fifteen."

"You saw her *leave* the gate?"

"You said '*one* last question,' but then you asked a second one. A five-dollar one, if I'm not mistaken."

I rummage around in my handbag till I find a five. When I hand it over he says, "I saw that pretty girl at Gate 15, heard her on the phone breaking up with some guy named Ron, watched her walk all the way down the hall to the movin' sidewalk."

"Did you happen to notice anyone following her?"

He points to my phone. "Not *this* man."

"But you *did* see someone following her?"

He looks around, lowers his voice. "White man. Business suit."

"Can you describe him?"

"Maybe."

"How much will *that* cost me?"

"What's it worth to you?"

"I won't know till I hear what you've got to say."

"You seem like an honest person," he says. "I'm thinkin' what little I know's worth another five. But if it's worth *more*, I'll trust you to pay the difference. How's that sound?"

"Sounds more than fair."

"I never saw his face, 'cause I was lookin' at her. But I couldn't help but see him slide right on in behind her, movin' real close. Stood behind her on the movin' sidewalk, like he was sniffin' her hair..." His voice trails off.

I wait for Stay Busy to say more, but he seems lost in thought. So I say, "Well, Mr. Busy, that's not much, but I'll pay you the five you thought it was worth, but only because you turned out to be charming after all."

"I ain't told you the five-dollar part yet," he says.

"You ain't?"

He says, "Thing I noticed that didn't look right, was his shoes."

"What about them?"

"He had on the suit, like I said, but on his feet was white Keds."

I do a double-take. "*Keds?* You're *sure?*"

"'Course I'm sure! You don't see men wearin' Keds every day. Not with a business suit."

I suddenly remember that, in addition to the Keds, Presley said all the junior high girls thought Quelvin was creepy because *he used to sniff their hair!*

I only have one fifty in my wallet, but have no hesitation giving it to Stay Busy the Porter, who holds it up to the lights with both hands and studies it till his face breaks into a wide grin. Then he shouts, "*Ulysses!* I ain't seen you since *Appomattox!* Where *have* you been, my man?"

I call Dillon while paying for my jelly beans. By the time he answers, I'm walking toward the parking garage. I tell him what Stay Busy said, but before he can properly praise me he says, "Just a sec, Dani, I'm on the phone with Presley's mother."

A moment later he says, "The police are taking Presley in for questioning."

"*What?* Tell her not to say a word till she gets a lawyer!"

"Her mom already told her. Now she's asking us to recommend an attorney."

In the middle of all this, Donovan Creed chooses this very moment to finally return my call.

"Call Barb!" I tell Dillon, then abruptly hang up and take Creed's call.

Though my heart's racing, I do my best to sound casual while saying:

Chapter 28

"ARE YOU TAKING A BREAK? Or have you already solved your case?"

"I don't have cases," Creed says. "But yeah, I solved someone's problem."

I know not to ask for clarification. When Creed solves someone's problem, he's not talking about restoring their hard drive.

"How can I help you?" he says.

"Did it ever occur to you I just called to say hi and see how things are going?"

"No."

"Why not?"

"Because you and I have a Level 2 friendship."

"I'm not familiar with that term," I say, "and quite frankly, I don't like the sound of it."

He laughs, but doesn't explain. So I ask, "What's a Level 2 friendship?"

"Level 2 is when you really like someone, and you'd do anything for them, within reason. It's the "within reason" part that prevents it from being Level 1."

"Give me a for instance."

"When something great happens in your life, who's the first person you'd call to tell?"

"Sophie."

"Let me clarify. Who's the first person you'd call that you're not banging?"

"Dillon."

"Then you and Dillon might have a Level 1 friendship."

"What's the rest of the criteria?"

"Would Dillon help you bury a body, no questions asked?"

"Um...no, probably not. I mean, he'd definitely ask questions about it."

"Then you and Dillon are Level 2. There are very few Level 1 friendships in the world that are reciprocated. Like you and me. I'm a Level 1 for you, but you're a 2 for me. If you asked me to blow up a building, or bury a body for you, I wouldn't hesitate. But you'd never do those things for me."

"I think you're selling me short. I might do those things for you. How can you automatically say I wouldn't?"

"You proved it just now, by saying you *might* do them. You'd need a reason. You'd ask questions. You might do them if you could *justify* it."

"Well, that's got to be better than a Level 2."

"Level 1 is like I have with Callie Carpenter, and used to have with Augustus Quinn, before he...passed away. This is the man or woman you can call without hesitation, knowing they'll break laws for you, as you would for them."

"I'd break laws to help you. I break laws all the time."

He laughs. "I'm not talking about fashion laws."

"You think that's funny?"

"I do, and my laughter proves it."

I raise my voice: "I insist on a higher ranking for our friendship."

"What do you suggest?"

"One-point-five."

"Very well. I'll remain your Level 1, and elevate you to a 1.5."

"Thank you."

He says, "Can I assume you're finally ready to tell me what you need?"

"If you insist. You've heard of WITSEC, the Witness Protection Program?"

"What about it?"

"I need to access their databases."

"Why?"

"I need to find out if someone's in Witness Protection. If so, I'd like to know his current name, address, and list of crimes he's committed. Also—"

—"That's not going to happen. I doubt three people in the world can access that data."

"I'm sure you've got contacts in the US Marshall's Service."

"I do," he says, "But I'm the last person they'd tell."

"Why?"

"Everyone in Witness Protection has the same problem: someone wants them dead. And brace yourself: there's a nasty rumor going around that I'm an assassin."

"So I've heard. But...it's just the US *Marshalls*, right? I'm sure *you* could breach their security."

"Thanks for the vote of confidence, but you should know there are people employed by the service whose sole purpose is to keep me and Callie Carpenter from learning the WITSEC identities, on the *chance* we might be interested in killing them. Even my geeks would have trouble accessing that data."

"Nevertheless, I *do* have confidence in your abilities, and I'd be shocked if you couldn't locate someone in WITSEC if you had to."

"*Had* to?"

"Yeah."

"If I *had* to—meaning, if my life depended on it—then...yeah, there's one person I could call. But it would mean calling in a favor."

"*Really?* That's *fantastic!*"

"Whoa! Slow down. What I'm saying—"

I interrupt: "If someone owed *me* a favor, and *you* needed help—"

He interrupts: "This is different. Trust me. This is a favor I can't afford to waste."

I frown. "How big could it possibly be?"

"Are you kidding me? *Huge!* Bigger than anything you can imagine."

"Maybe it's time to collect."

"You're not following. The favor he owes is beyond your capacity to comprehend."

"Are you sure you're not overstating?"

"Quite sure. You could write a *book* about the favor he owes me. This is what I call an Ultimate Favor."

"Got it. He owes you a big favor. I understand."

Creed sighs.

"It would be for a good cause," I say.

"No offense, Dani, but I doubt you could champion a cause worthy of this favor."

"I think you're wrong. You're a crusader, Donovan, and this is the noblest of causes."

"I can't imagine anything you can say that would make me call in this particular favor. But...I've always had a soft spot for you, so...go ahead. Tell me what you hope to achieve."

I take a deep breath. Then say, "You'd be helping me stop a serial rapist."

The line goes so quiet I fear he's hung up on me. But then he says, "I don't mean to sound insensitive, Dani, especially given your history. But that's not even *close* to hitting the mark."

"You'd let this bastard continue to rape innocent women?"

"That's a harsh way to put it. I'm not *letting* him do anything."

"If you could stop him, but *don't*, it's the same as letting him continue."

"You're blaming *me* for what this man does? By extension, am I responsible for *every* rape that occurs?"

"Every rape you could prevent."

"If I were in the right place at the right time I could prevent them *all*. But since a new rape occurs in this country every—how many seconds?"

"Forty-six."

"Exactly. So we're talking what, seventy-eight rapes per hour?"

"Uh..." I try to work it out in my head, but give up. "I'll trust you to do the math."

"Well, I think you'll agree it's asking a lot to expect me to prevent them all."

"You could prevent all the ones *this* man will commit."

"I appreciate your passion, Dani. But I have to say no."

"Seriously?" He's saying no? He's never said no to me before.

"I'm sorry," he adds.

I'm stunned. Not sure how to respond. Finally come up with, "It's...okay, Donovan."

"Are we still friends?"

"Of course. We'll *always* be friends, far as I'm concerned. And like you said, you've been a better friend to me than I've been to you. You've always been there for me, always accepted my calls. And even now, you listened to me, and let me make my case. I just wish I understood you a little better."

"In what way?"

"A while ago you said you were a Level 1 friend to me, even though I'm just a Level 1.5 to you. You said the difference between us was that a Level 1 friend would do anything for the other person, no questions asked."

"I think if you could replay our conversation you'd remember I said a Level 1 friend would help you bury a body, or break a law, no questions asked."

"Isn't that the same thing?"

"No. Ultimate Favors go way beyond friendship levels."

"Okay, that helps. I think I understand."

"You probably don't, but like I said, it's a no. I'm really sorry. Goodbye."

"*Wait!*" I shout.

"Aw shit," he says.

I try one last time: "There must be something I can say or do to talk you into making that call."

"I can only think of one thing. And trust me, you don't want to do it."

"What would I have to do?"

"Replace the favor."

"What does that mean?"

"You'd owe me the same favor I'm calling in."

"Done!" I say. "I'll owe you the Ultimate Favor instead of the guy."

"It's not worth it, Dani. I'm telling you right now, it's a bad bargain."

"I don't care! I'll do it! I'll owe you the favor."

"You clearly have no idea what you're offering."

"Then...tell me in a way I'll understand."

Chapter 29

"LIKE I SAID, AN ULTIMATE FAVOR goes beyond a Level 1 friendship," Creed explains. "In other words, I would never ask Callie to do what I'll *expect* you to do."

"I'm listening."

"Before I give you some examples, you need to know that if you agree to assume this man's favor, it means when I need you, you'll have to drop whatever you're doing and perform whatever task I ask of you."

"No problem."

"Think again, Dani."

"About what?"

"I'm Donovan Creed."

"So?"

"I'm not sure you can comprehend the type of favor I might ask. And make no mistake: I might love you, but refusing the favor is not an option."

"I'm okay with that. You know why? Because I know *you*. You wouldn't ask something of me that's unreasonable."

"You just proved you have no idea what I'm saying."

"Then give me an example."

"The favor could be anything, but it won't be small."

"For the love of *God*, Donovan, give me an *example!*"

"Very well. I might call you one night and tell you to set Sophie on fire while she sleeps, for no other reason than to get you into a maximum security prison so you can try to kill a dangerous inmate. If you fail, you're dead. If you succeed, you'll be in prison for the rest of your life."

"You can't be serious."

"Maybe I'll need you to serve as a human guinea pig for a chemical weapon. Or I might call you one day and require your heart for an emergency transplant for one of my employees."

"What?"

"*These* are simple, off-the-cuff examples. It would almost certainly be something far worse."

"How could anything be worse?"

"Maybe I'll inject you with a deadly, but highly contagious virus and put you to work in an overseas whorehouse frequented by known terrorists. You'd live for about a week, in the worst agony imaginable, during which time your goal would be to have sex with at least forty men, including, hopefully, a number of terrorists, who would then infect their friends, relatives, and associates. You'd feel badly for the hundreds of innocent children who'll die as a direct result of your actions, but you'll be happy knowing you saved tens of thousands of others, who would have died from future terrorist attacks. Unless you didn't happen to infect *any* terrorists, in which case you'll have murdered hundreds, possibly *thousands*, of innocent people for nothing. Want another example?"

Before I can say no, he says, "Maybe I'll need you to strap on a suicide vest, walk into a public building, and blow yourself up, along with hundreds of innocent Americans."

"*Why* on earth would you have me do *that?*"

"Maybe Homeland needs a budget increase, or wants to influence privacy laws. Maybe the government has decided to shut down our division and needs a reason not to."

"You're being ridiculous. The Donovan Creed I know wouldn't kill innocent people in order to secure additional funding."

"What if that funding was essential to saving the city of Nashville?"

"Well..."

"In World War II, the British broke the German's messaging code long before the war was over, but couldn't let word get out, or the Germans would have changed the code. If that happened, the British and Allies wouldn't be able to use their intelligence to win the major battles. So time and again the British had to allow ships to be sunk that they could have saved. Someone had to make the decision to allow thousands of servicemen to die in order to save millions of citizens and shorten the war. These are tough decisions, and the type I deal with daily."

"How do you sleep at night?"

"With one eye open."

"Can you give me any examples that don't require me to die, or spend the rest of my life in prison?"

"I could give you many, but I doubt you'd want to hear them, since you'd probably never sleep again. This is what I mean by an Ultimate Favor. Any questions?"

"You'd really ask me to do those types of things, knowing I'd be killed, maimed, or imprisoned for *life*?"

"I wouldn't *ask* you, Dani. I'd demand it. Now, once and for all: do you really want to take the man's place and owe me his Ultimate Favor?"

"No."

"So you're going to let that guy in Witness Protection continue to rape innocent women?"

"I am. And his victims can damn me for eternity. Sorry."

"Don't be. It just means you finally understand what I've been trying to explain."

"Got it. Can I ask *you* a question?"

"Anything."

"What…in the name of God…did you do for this guy that he'd be willing to do an Ultimate Favor for you?"

"I saved his village from a nuclear explosion."

"He owns a *village*?"

"He's from Bavaria," Creed says, as if that's explanation enough. Then, just as we're about to hang up, he shocks the shit out of me by saying…

Chapter 30

"WHAT WAS THE GUY'S NAME?"

"Huh?"

"The guy in WITSEC," Creed says. "The rapist. What's his last known name?"

"James Quelvin." I spell it for him, then say, "Last known address, Tallahassee, Florida. Last known occupation, Junior high school teacher."

"You're sure he's in Witness Protection?"

"No, but pretty sure. Why are you asking?"

"It strikes me that if I call the Bavarian village guy, he's going to be terrified."

"*I* would be."

"If I tell him I'm not calling about the favor, he might be so relieved he'd be willing to tell me if Quelvin's in the Witness Protection program."

"That would be incredible!" I say.

"I can't make any promises, but I'll give it a shot."

"Omigod! Thank you!"

"Sorry if I frightened you earlier."

"It's okay. I had it coming. You're right. I had no idea."

Ten minutes later Creed calls me back.

Too quick. I'm devastated.

I know exactly what he's going to say, but it hurts even worse than I expected: "Sorry Dani. I've got nothing for you. My guy's never heard of Quelvin."

"It's okay, Donovan. The fact that you tried…well, it means a lot. Thank you for trying."

"You're so very welcome," he says. "By the way, I'm kidding."

"Huh?"

"You won't *believe* what I've got for you!"

"Omigod! I love you!"

"How could you not?"

"Tell me!" I say.

"You were right. James Quelvin *is* in Witness Protection. But his name's been changed."

"To what?"

"I don't know."

"Is he living in Nashville?"

"Again, I don't know. I didn't want to call in the favor. But I can tell you enough to curl your hair."

"Shit."

"What's wrong?"

"I hate curly hair. Can you just tell me enough to make it wavy?"

Creed laughs.

I ask, "What did he do to get into WITSEC, testify against the mob?"

"He *did* agree to testify against the mob, though it hasn't happened yet, for various reasons. But guess what forced him to turn state's evidence?"

"He raped a student."

"He did. But not just *one* student."

"How many?"

"Nine. Over nine years. And get this: on his birthday!"

"When's his birthday?"

"When do you think?"

"Last Sunday?"

"You got it!"

"But—"

"What's wrong?"

"The odds of him being in Nashville last Sunday, and raping a young lady he happens to see in an airport, who turns out to be his former student from Tallahassee—have to be a trillion to one."

"If you look at it that way, I'd have to agree," Creed says. "But you're looking at it backwards."

"What do you mean?"

"This Quelvin character might be the most insidious bastard who ever lived."

"Why?"

"I have a list of the girls he raped."

"And?"

"The first student he ever raped was...Presley Ayers."

"Omigod!"

"Can we assume your client's maiden name is Ayers?"

"Omigod! You're saying he raped Presley when she was twelve?"

"That's right. And he tracked her down and raped her again, ten years later."

"Omigod!"

Chapter 31

MY HEART'S DOING CARTWHEELS! I almost shout the next question: "Who's the second girl he raped?"

"Alice Sims."

"He's going to rape her next year, on his birthday!"

"No he's not."

"Of *course* he is! It's a *pattern!*"

"He's not going to rape her because I'll be waiting for him."

"You're going to kill him?"

"Let's just say I'm going to protect Alice, and leave it at that."

"We don't have to wait a year, Donovan, we can get him right now! All we have to do is turn this information over to the police. With Presley's rape kit evidence and eyewitness testimony, they can match his DNA, arrest him, prosecute him, and put him away forever."

"That *sounds* great, Dani, but it's not how the system works. If Presley's rape gets prosecuted, the DNA evidence will magically disappear. And even if it doesn't, when Quelvin finds out we're onto him, he'll change his M.O."

"Not prosecuting the rape goes against everything I believe in. There must be some way to preserve the evidence, some way to get Quelvin. If the Marshalls are forced to turn him over…"

"He's in WITSEC, Dani. Whatever crimes he commits will be covered up or placed in limbo until he finally testifies. The Marshalls will keep changing his name, keep relocating him, and the girls will keep getting raped."

"Every year. On his birthday."

"At this point, that's what we hope. But we sure as hell don't want the Marshalls connecting the dots like we did. Because if they figure out this birthday thing they'll sit on him next year and make sure he doesn't go anywhere. If that happens, Quelvin will change his M.O. and start going after new women. He might *never* get caught."

"I think we have a problem," I say.

"What's that?"

"It took you no time at all to connect the dots about the rapes occurring on his birthday, and you did it based on the information your contact gave."

"So?"

"The Marshalls will also be able to connect the dots."

"Only if they find out he raped Presley for the second time. And they won't learn that if Presley fails to prosecute him."

"But if he's raping all these girls on his birthday, surely they'll be able to—"

"Like all law enforcement agencies, the Marshalls are understaffed. Their job is to protect witnesses, not search for criminal evidence against them."

"What if Quelvin finds out we're onto him?"

"That can only happen if you tell someone, because you, me, and Quelvin are the only people in the world who know about this. And *I'm* obviously not going to tell anyone."

"Me either."

"Can you keep this a secret?"

"For a year? Absolutely!"

"Actually, you'd have to keep it forever, because the Marshalls won't be happy to lose their star witness. If word got out that you knew this man was going to die on his birthday, they could put you in prison for the rest of your life."

"What about you?"

"They won't be able to put me at the scene."

"What if they torture me into giving up your name?"

He laughs. "They won't. But even if you name me, Quelvin is giving me a whole year to prepare an alibi!"

"Donovan? I know this is good, but it's also terrible!"

"Why?"

"Presley will never know we got him."

"So?"

"She'll think we failed her."

"Dani?"

"Yeah?"

"Don't tell Presley!"

"Okay. But...can I help you bury Quelvin's body?"

He chuckles. "This isn't your type of gig."

"I know. But I'd still like to help you bury him. Especially after what you said about Level 1 friends. You've always been there for me, and I want to do the same."

"Thanks."

"You're welcome."

"We don't actually bury the bodies, Dani."

"What?"

"That was a figure of speech."

"Oh. But still, whatever it is you do, I want to—"

"Dani?"

"Yeah?"

"Relax. I got this."

"Okay. Thank you."

"You really want to thank me?"

"I do."

"Then don't tell Presley!"

"You keep saying that. Don't worry, I won't."

After hanging up, I turn my attention to Dillon, who's been calling the whole time I was talking to Creed. I couldn't take a chance on dropping the call, so I ignored him. Now he's on the phone saying, "What the fuck?"

"Sorry, Dillon. I was on the phone with Creed."

"And?"

"He can't help us."

"Shit."

"I know, right?"

After a moment of silence he says, "Have you seen it on TV?"

"What's that?"

"The FAA finally admitted they recovered the black box from the plane crash."

"What took them so long?"

"Guess they wanted to analyze the flight recording first."

"And have they?"

"Oh yeah!"

"And what are they saying about it?"

"You honestly don't know?"

"If I did I wouldn't keep asking. But if you don't hurry up and tell me I *will* cut off your pink, hairless nuts and dunk them in my fish tank."

"You don't have a fish tank."

"I'll buy one."

"Can I help you pick it out?"

"That seems only fair, given the circumstances. Now quit fucking around and tell me why I should give a shit what they found on the flight recorder."

"Okay, but prepare to say holy shit."

"I can assure you I won't say that."

"Not only will you say it...you'll *mean* it!"

"How can a person *mean* holy shit?"

"You'll see."

"Enough! What did they announce?"

"Ron the Pilot's last words."

"And what were they?"

"He said, '*This is for you, Presley!*'"

"Holy *shit!*"

John Locke

"Told you!"

Chapter 32

I DIDN'T JUST LIE A FEW MINUTES AGO...I LIED TO DONOVAN CREED!

I stood there, on the phone, and told him—big as you please!—that I'd *never* tell Presley we cracked the case, and that Quelvin was going to die next year on his birthday.

I lied to Donovan Creed!

But—and this might prove huge later on, in the event he considers killing me over it—I never *promised* I wouldn't tell her.

You'll think I'm splitting hairs, and maybe Creed will, too, but to me, breaking a promise is far worse than telling a lie.

But maybe that's because I lie all the time.

Mostly, I lie about small stuff, like, "I *love* your hair!" or, "No, *really*! That gown looks *perfect* on you!" But sometimes it's about bigger stuff, like, "You're the best lover I ever had!" or, "I can't *believe* you didn't see me in church! Where were you *sitting?*" Also, I find it easier to lie to friends ("Don't worry, Donovan, I'll never tell Presley that Quelvin's going to die next year!") than to strangers: ("What do you *mean* you didn't get my payment? That's *crazy!* Not only did I *write* the check, I *personally* handed it to the mail carrier!")

I *assured* Creed I wouldn't tell Presley, and though he probably took my assurance as a promise, I was very careful not to say the words: "I promise I'll never tell Presley."

—Because I had every intention of telling her, right from the start!

Sorry if this puts a thorn in your paw, Donovan, but from the moment I learned Quelvin raped her ten years ago, all bets were off.

I was willing to lie to Creed just this once because I know something about Presley he could never understand: the extent to which she's mentally flawed.

Presley "sees" Quelvin wherever she goes, even when he's not there. If this poor girl can't distinguish a nose-less face from a normal one, or a white man from a black man, she's got more problems than Gringott's has goblins. And those problems will return each year. If Creed kills Quelvin next year and Presley isn't allowed to know about it, her symptoms will start up again, and she'll continue seeing Quelvin. And this will almost certainly go on year after year, for the rest of her life.

If I don't tell Presley she's safe, no one will.

She's twice a victim already, but additionally, for the past ten years her mind has forced her to keep "seeing" him, and reliving the events over and over, like some annual version of Bill Murray's *Groundhog Day*—with none of the fun parts.

Quelvin haunts her thoughts, and will continue doing so till she's absolutely convinced he's dead. Not to tell her it's over would be the cruelest thing imaginable. She, of all people, deserves to know that her horrors—and Quelvin's reign of terror—are finally over. Only when she's convinced she's safe, can the healing process begin.

That's my take on the subject, and if I wind up losing Creed's friendship because I told her, then that's how it will have to be.

Moments ago I spoke to Presley on the phone, to let her know I was on my way to the police department. She said the detectives were making her wait in the interrogation room till her attorney arrived, so I reminded her not to joke around, or mug for the camera, or say anything to anyone. I told her Barb would be there soon, and assured her she's the best attorney I know.

I wasn't lying about Barb.

Barbara "Barb" Allen is a 300-pound feminist pit bull who looks like a cross between Andre the Giant and Custer's Last Stand. She's King Kong on a bad day, with a shrimp and grits complexion and less charm than a beached mullet. She specializes in the complete and thorough evisceration of police officers.

Presley said her mom was in the waiting room, and asked if I could entertain her, so she wouldn't go up to some stranger and say something stupid that could get Presley in trouble. I said I'd be glad to, and asked what her mom looks like, and she said she didn't know.

"You don't know what your mom looks like?"

"Not off-hand," she said. "Not in a way I can describe, like hair color, or features. But you'll know her when you see her."

Fortunately, Jean Ayers is easy to spot, being by far the prettiest woman in the room, and the biggest artificially-chested woman I've ever seen in person. I introduce myself, and she immediately informs me that Presley is crazier than bat shit, and needs to be committed.

"What makes you think she's crazy?" I ask.

"She sometimes spends the entire day hiding in closets and other cubbies she's made, like behind the washing machine, or inside the cabinet of her wet bar. At night she sleeps on the floor under her bed, and even did it when she and Mitch were married! You know how we always knew when it was close to President's Day in our house? That's the time of year Presley always thinks her junior high school teacher is stalking her. Need more examples? She can't recognize *me*—her own *mother*—and probably couldn't pick me out of a three-person lineup. So yeah, I think she's crazy. You want to talk about bad judgment?"

I shrug.

Jean says, "She married a man who couldn't support her lifestyle, and didn't even bother to get herself named on his life insurance policy! I told her no one's as poor as that worthless piece of shit claimed to be. 'He's hiding money somewhere,' I told her, and said we need to get a forensic accountant to find out what the fuck's going on. And an attorney, so she can contest that insurance policy bullshit. But you know what she said? 'Let it go!' Can you *believe* that shit?"

The entrance door suddenly flies open, and Barb Allen storms through the room like a cyclone with a grudge. "Be with you in a minute," she says, breezing past me. She suddenly stops, looks over her shoulder at Jean and says, "You too, Miss Titts."

We watch a trembling policeman escort Barb through the door that leads to the interrogation room. When it closes, Jean says, "What the fuck was that?"

"Presley's attorney."

"Man, woman, or beast?"

"Woman."

"You're sure about that?"

"Positive."

"Well, I think she's a lesbian."

I feel like slapping the piss out of her, then slapping her again, for pissing. But I settle for changing the subject.

"Presley's been through a lot," I say.

"Oh, boo hoo!" she says. "You know what *I* say? 'Suck it up!' You know what Presley's problem is? She's a quitter. A crybaby. She's got no ambition. Always takes the easy way out, like her father, the fuckwad."

"I like her," I say.

"Of *course* you do! She's gorgeous! But do you think she uses that to her advantage? Hell no! I tell her she needs to get what she can while the getting's good. She won't look like this forever. Right now she's as ripe as she's ever going to be. In a few years, the rot will show—we're *all* rotting, you know. I'm rotting, you're rotting, and Presley will be, too, before she knows it—and it's a downhill battle from there. I'm living proof of that. You seen any of my movies?"

I give her a closer look. The answer's no, but I don't want to be rude, so I say, "You look awfully familiar…"

"Damn right I do. And I had to work my ass off for every piece of shit role I ever got. But Presley? She wouldn't spread her legs for God himself. Just that loser she married." She assumes a little girl's voice and says, "*I need to love a man before I'll sleep with him.*" Then she says, "You believe that shit? Starlets would *kill* to look like her. As for *casting* directors? Hell, at her age I'd had more dicks in me than the porta-potty at Oktoberfest. And I wasn't *half* as good-looking as she is!"

I try to wipe the shocked expression off my face, but since that's not possible, I concentrate on closing my gaping mouth. No wonder her daughter's got issues. After three minutes with this bitch I'm ready to jump off the nearest bridge.

I ask, "Has Presley ever seen a psychiatrist?"

"Of course. Lots of them. And they think she's crazy, too!"

"Was she ever diagnosed?"

"*Diagnosed?*" She laughs. "Of *course* she was! How else could they justify wiping out my life's savings?"

"What did they say she suffers from?"

"Fregoli something-or-other."

"What's that?"

"Typical psychiatric bullshit. You call that a profession? It's a racket! You know what I say?"

"What's that?"

"I say there's no such thing as mental problems. You either suck it up or quit. You stay in motion or stop, drop, and dig your grave."

I smile, reach into my bag, and say, "Would you care for a jelly bean? They're super fresh. I just got them twenty minutes ago."

"Just a few," she says. "I'm watching my figure. Because if *I* don't, who will?"

"Who, indeed?" I say.

As Jean nibbles her candy, Barb bursts through the door, with Presley in tow. I jump to my feet, but Barb says, "Not here. We'll talk outside."

Jean and I follow them outside, and within seconds they're mobbed by a swarm of reporters and angry friends and relatives of plane crash victims, shouting and cursing at Presley. In the midst of all this commotion, I happen to catch sight of a man pushing his way toward the front. There's something wrong here, something about the way he's... I suddenly notice the gun in his hand, but before I can shout out a warning, he fires two shots, and Presley goes down.

Chapter 33

THE FIRST BULLET CAUGHT PRESLEY HIGH, in the shoulder, and spun her around. It's the spinning that saved her life, and the sole reason Jack Kraft's second shot missed its target.

Now, six hours later, the whole world knows Kraft's wife and kids perished in the plane crash. According to Barb, the reporters and protesters learned she'd been taken to the police station because a rookie cop posted the news on Instagram.

"That's a lawsuit right there," I tell Presley, but she waves my words away with her good arm. "The officer's my age," she says. "He made a rookie mistake. I could never sue the police for that."

Nor is Presley in any trouble with the police. As Barb explained on national TV, "You can't prosecute a person for breaking up with her boyfriend. If you could, we'd all be in prison. Well, perhaps not me," she said, chuckling. "And for those of you saying Presley knew Ron was depressed, and she broke up with him hoping he'd crash the plane so she could collect on his life insurance policy? Suck on this: his ex-wife's the sole beneficiary, and *has* been since the day it was written. And it's $200,000, not a million. Can we *finally* put this insanity behind us and let this poor girl start healing?"

The consensus was, America could.

Now, finally, it's just me and Presley in her hospital room. She's woozy, but lucid. After exchanging comments about her condition, she says, "You keep looking at the door like we're about to be interrupted. Is there something you want to tell me in private?"

I bite my bottom lip and spit it out: "You were raped ten years ago."

She says nothing.

"By James Quelvin," I add.

When she fails to respond, I say, "That's a pretty important detail to omit, don't you think?"

She turns her face toward the window and remains quiet a long time before saying, "How'd you find out?"

I take a deep breath, swear her to secrecy, then tell her every word of my conversation with Donovan Creed. When I'm finished, she says, "Barb wants to prosecute the rape."

Of course she does.

Shit.

"You'll have to tell her you changed your mind."

"I agree. But with all these reporters..."

She's right. The police report's been filed, the rape kit completed. It's going to get out, which means Presley's evidence will get lost, or compromised, Quelvin will be relocated, the Marshalls will connect the dots, keep him on a short leash each year around the date of his birthday, and we'll never get him.

She says, "Do you think Creed's tough enough to kill Quelvin?"

I laugh. "Creed's tough enough to kill the entire Marshalls' Service."

She shows me a half grin. "Think he'd be willing to throw in my mom?"

I say, "If not, I'll kill her myself!"

Next morning, it requires a signed consent letter, and a Face Time consultation with Presley herself, before psychiatrist Dr. Ann Compton agrees to discuss Presley's condition with me.

"Presley suffers from a form of Fregoli delusion," she says.

"Which is what, exactly?"

"It's a rare disorder in which a person believes he or she is being persecuted by someone who can change appearance or disguise himself to others. In Presley's case, she can see several different people and be convinced it's the same person."

"You're saying if Presley and I look at the same person, she sees the bad guy, but thinks he's disguising his looks to me?"

"Correct. In your example, she'd think you're the one being tricked, not her. It's not only frustrating, but...terrifying for her."

"Did she ever tell you about James Quelvin?"

"Of course. He's the man she accused of raping her at age twelve, though she didn't report it until a year later, when she began "seeing" him in places he couldn't be. After accusing three different men of being the man who raped her, she insisted it was, in fact, Mr. Quelvin, her seventh-grade English teacher who committed the crime. Of course, by that time the police considered him nothing more than the fourth person she'd named, and, being a year late to the party, there was no *proof* of sexual assault, so charges were never brought. Quelvin continued to teach, and Presley's family moved to Memphis, where I began treating her, then to Nashville, after she had accused nine different men of having raped her over a four-year period. Every year, around the anniversary of her alleged rape, she believes she sees him at every turn."

"Presley looked into the face of a man with no nose and believed him to be Quelvin."

"Interesting. How did the man lose his nose?"

I perk up. "Does that make a difference somehow?"

"No. I was just curious."

"Me too! It's been driving me *crazy*! I've actually snapped at people for no reason over this very issue. Not only that, but I can't sleep at night, for worrying about it."

"Worrying?"

"I even called him on the phone and offered to tell him my deepest, darkest secret if he'd tell me what happened to his nose, but he refused."

"I see. Can I ask you a personal question?"

"Of course."

"Are you currently seeing anyone in Nashville?"

"Wow! That *is* personal! I have to say, I'm flattered. But to be completely honest, yes. I'm seeing a wonderful young lady named Sophie Alexander."

"How young?"

"Mid-twenties."

Dr. Compton pauses a moment. "Sophie Alexander, you say?"

"Yes."

"I'm not familiar with that name. Are you seeing her regularly?"

"I am. In fact, we're virtually inseparable."

"I see. And would you say she's fulfilling your needs?"

"Wow! Again, that's pretty forward!"

"I'm not trying to make you uncomfortable, it's just that I'm not sure this Sophie person is right for you."

"What do you mean?"

"I'd like you to consider meeting a close friend of mine, Mabel Longtree. She's an outstanding person, and a highly-respected therapist."

"You mean like a *massage* therapist? Omigod, Sophie would shit!"

"I'd be glad to arrange a meeting, if you like. Sophie wouldn't have to know."

"Well, I probably shouldn't tell you this, but I strayed from Sophie once before, and it went really badly. I'm super lucky she took me back."

"Well, if you change your mind..."

"That is just so *sweet* of you! Your friend sounds wonderful, but like I say, I'm seeing Sophie, and things are going great. But if that changes, I'll be sure to give you a call, and maybe you can introduce me to your friend at that time, if she's still available."

"For *you*, I'm certain she'd be available."

"Why, *thank* you, Doctor! I'm honored."

"Well...you're welcome. Did you have any other questions about Presley?"

"I do. She identified a black man as being James Quelvin."

"That's not unusual. Any face she perceives as being similar to Quelvin's, however her mind defines that—will manifest in her brain as being him. And she'll believe it with total certainty."

I think about that a minute, then say, "If something were to happen to Quelvin, like maybe he gets arrested for something, and he's tried, convicted, and sentenced to life imprisonment, would that break the chain? Would Presley stop seeing him in other people's faces each year?"

"I don't think so."

"Why not?"

"Her internal clock is triggered to see him every year. Even if she knows he's in prison, I think she'd see his face and believe he somehow escaped."

"What if he died?"

"That might do it. But only if she were absolutely convinced."

"Can I ask you one more question? The things you've said, I totally understand. But what I don't understand is why Presley can't recognize—or even *describe*—her own mother."

"Don't get me started on the mother!" she said, so I didn't. But after talking to Dr. Compton, I'm convinced if Creed had been able to *kill* Quelvin, and could have proved it to Presley, she'd be cured of this awful Fregoli delusion.

Fregoli delusion?

Jeez Trapeze!

I take a minute to wonder how many maladies and aberrations there are in the world, and before I realize it, my mind goes to Butter Man, the homeless guy who hangs out on the sidewalk in front of our office building every day. The Butter Man suffers from some sort of delusion that makes him think he's at a fancy banquet 24/7, and constantly needs butter for his roll.

"Gimme some butter," he says to all who pass him on the sidewalk. Then he'll say, "I'm the guest speaker. You can't have this banquet without me. It's in my honor. All I'm askin' for's a pat of butter. You seen my picture in the lobby? This is *my* event! I been travelin' all day. Airports and airplanes, nothin' to eat. Gimme some butter. I'm the guest speaker. You can't have this banquet without me...."

I've heard him say these words a thousand times, and never any others. I've given him food, water, spare change, the occasional blanket...but he never stops talking about the pat of butter someone's not giving him.

I tell Presley what Dr. Compton said, and then, in order to make her feel better, I tell her at least she's not homeless, and crazy, like the Butter Man, and that, unlike him, at least her issues are solvable.

When she asks, "Who's the Butter Man?" I tell her the whole story, including all the wonderful things I've done for him. Without batting an eye, she says, "Did you ever think to just give him a pat of butter?"

Chapter 34

TEN DAYS LATER, everything has changed. Not only has Presley recovered from the shooting, she's also become one of the wealthiest women in America!

Her transformation from poor to wealthy began the moment the authorities aired Ron's final words: *This is for you, Presley!* –and hasn't let up since.

The media's been eating it up because as a news story, it's got everything: a gorgeous girl. A plane crash. A lover's triangle. A shooting. Not to mention...well, you get the picture:

It's got everything.

But most of all it has Presley, one of the most unassuming and beautiful young women the world has ever seen, who appeared on the national stage, literally, out of nowhere. On looks alone, half the country idolizes her. On name alone, every former and current Elvis Presley fan adores her. The entire country of France—and French-speaking people everywhere—are celebrating her *Surname!*

Of course there were millions who initially blamed her for having the affair that caused the plane crash that killed 93 innocent people. But the talking heads and pundits hammered home the message that Presley broke off the relationship with Ron to go back to her husband. They also pointed out if the airline didn't understand the depths of Ron's depression issues, how could Presley be expected to know? The result being that most of her haters began seeing her in a different light. It also helped her cause when live videos recorded at her shooting revealed her shouting to the crowd: "Please don't hurt him!"

How could America hate this gorgeous, courageous young lady who urged people not to hurt the man who just shot and tried to kill her?

They couldn't.

Those who hadn't succumbed to Presley's charm the first few days after her shooting came around after learning she'd been brutally raped in the aftermath of the plane crash that caused the death of her lover and her husband.

Within days, the Presley French story became the biggest news story since 9/11. Just today I saw a special feature where a news team was putting mikes in people's faces, asking where they were and what they were doing when they heard Presley had been shot.

Newspapers. Magazines. Radio talk shows. TV talk shows. *Entertainment Tonight. Inside Edition. TMZ. Access Hollywood.* Late night comedians. Bloggers. Opinion makers. Trend spotters. Politicians. Singers. Movie stars.

Entertainers. You name it, they spoke her name with reverence. When she publicly turned down a multi-million dollar offer from an adult magazine to appear nude within their pages she was endorsed and embraced by churches and women's groups alike.

Agents and PR firms battled tooth and nail to represent her. Magazines and book publishers engaged in fierce bidding wars to secure her exclusive photos and story. Advertisers clamored to make her the face of their products, knowing if Presley could be seen drinking their soft drink, using their lipstick, wearing their clothes, eating their food, driving their car—it could be worth tens of millions of dollars in sales.

Before her first public appearance, Hollywood's top actors were sending extravagant gifts, jockeying for the opportunity to be seen publicly escorting her from the hospital. One A-lister privately offered to divorce his wife of twelve years if Presley would agree to tell the press they had started dating, and he might be "the one."

As the insanity raged on, Presley, being herself, could do no wrong. Everything she said endeared her to the public that much more, including: "Thank you for the offer, but I'd prefer not to pose nude. But I love your work." And, "No, I'm not criticizing those who appear nude. I don't believe in criticizing anybody." And, "Thanks for the offers, but I'm not really attracted to super-hot models, Hollywood actors, or men of wealth. I believe there are lots of average-looking men with average jobs who'd be fun to date and someday, possibly marry. Of course, that's a long way in the future, since I'm still mourning the loss of my husband, and feeling guilty for how I treated him before realizing how important he was to me. I've grown up a lot in the last few weeks, and hope to honor Mitch's memory by trying to be a better person."

The press ate it up. Everything she said—or didn't say—made news, but no one could have predicted how the Internet would affect her popularity.

Less than two hours after the NTSB and FAA confirmed Ron the Pilot's last words, skater dudes, extreme sports stars, hang gliders, street jumpers, and rooftop ninjas began posting the wildest, craziest, most death-defying videos ever seen, all of which started with the daredevil facing the camera and saying, "This is for you, Presley!" -And then performing the deed. Kids in school videoed themselves taking lesser dares, like holding up a school lunch item and saying, "This is for you, Presley!" and then consuming it.

By the end of the first day, "This is for you, Presley!" had become the most popular catch phrase in the history of the Internet.

By day two, gamblers in Vegas were spotted putting all their chips on the line, saying, "This is for you, Presley." Soccer moms, at restaurants, videoed themselves ordering a giant desert and saying, with fork or spoon poised, "This is for you, Presley."

On day three a dad posted a video of his 3-year-old daughter's birthday party, where she said, "This is for you, Presley," before blowing out the candles. It garnered 40 million views in twenty-four hours. The line was picked up by comedians and talk show hosts, who said it before going on stage. But when the president of the United States opened up a news conference with, "This is for you, Presley," she—Presley French, while still recuperating in the hospital—had become the most famous person on the planet Earth.

By the time she left the hospital, deals had been signed, and money exchanged. There would be a Presley doll, a fragrance, a clothing line, a car commercial, a TV reality show, a movie deal, a book contract, a rock album, and a coveted role as a judge on the top-rated talent show in the USA.

You can't make this shit up, people!

I'm happy for her, but I worry. Now that her rape has become public knowledge, it's only a matter of hours or days before the revelations go public about her fixation with James Quelvin, her former teacher, and how she's accused over a dozen innocent men of raping her over the years. While I'm sure her public relations team will be able to spin it positive, by making her a spokesperson for rape victims and Fregoli delusion sufferers around the world, I fear Presley will never be cured, since Creed won't be able to ambush Quelvin. And even if he could somehow find and kill Quelvin, we'd never be able to prove it to Presley's satisfaction. So I especially worry what will happen next year, on the anniversary of her sexual assaults. Will she accuse her manager of raping her? Her publicist? Her co-stars? Will she continue to live in fear? Will she eventually go off the deep end, or be driven to suicide?

So like I say, I worry.

But first things first: Presley's ready to leave the hospital and needs a safe place to stay. I offer her Sophie's house, and she accepts. This decision turns out to be very important because it puts Presley and me in the same place at the same time when a helicopter lands in the field behind Sophie's house at 2 a.m., and four special forces-type guys force the reporters, camera crews, fruitcakes, weirdoes, and well-wishers in our yard to clear a wide path for us, as we make our way to the smaller of two choppers.

Doesn't matter that half the crowd is following us, long as they don't impede us, and they don't.

We lift off, go high into the night sky, and travel 40 minutes without speaking.

I have no idea where we're going, or what we're doing. I only know that Donovan Creed called me ten minutes before take off and said, "My men are waiting for you at the front door. Bring Presley."

"How should we dress?" I asked, but the line was already dead.

In Creed's world, he gets to say shit like "Bring Presley," and everyone knows what it means: it means Sophie has to stay home. In Creed's world, no other explanations are necessary. I bet Creed tells his wife: "I've gotta go," and she knows not to ask "Where? With whom? When will you be back?" He probably just says "See you!" and takes off into the night sky.

Unfortunately, I don't live in Creed's world. I have a girlfriend who's quite possessive, which is understandable, since I recently broke her heart and lost her trust by having a brief affair with the aforementioned Beth Conroy.

Not my finest moment.

But even *before* the affair, Sofe would have been furious to see me and a sexy young lady like Presley going off in the middle of the night with no explanation, escorted by Creed's goons, heading toward a helicopter. She cussed us from the moment I got the call to the moment we walked out the door. By the time we buckled our seat belts, she'd sent 12 angry texts. Her last two made me laugh out loud:

Really Dani? After all that's happened you're flying away with Perfect Presley in a fucking helicopter? Like the bachelor on some fucking fantasy date? FUCK YOU!

And...

If you spend the night with her in some sort of fantasy suite, don't bother coming home! I will change the locks and throw all your personal shit on the lawn. Hope you enjoy yourself as much as the reporters and perverts who'll be sniffing your panties at 8am, which is exactly six hours from now!

I expect she's still texting, but I won't know till later, as Creed's pilot has confiscated our phones and handbags.

Chapter 35

WHEN THE CHOPPER EVENTUALLY LANDS, Presley asks, "Where are we?"

"In the middle of somewhere," I say.

I would have said "in the middle of *nowhere*," but that's a silly expression, since every place is obviously somewhere. Still, if you're looking for a place that could pass for nowhere, we just found it. And it's so secluded I wouldn't even consider getting out of the chopper if the guy approaching us wasn't—

"Is that him?" Presley says.

"Yup. That's Donovan Creed. Please tell me he doesn't look like Quelvin to you."

"I haven't seen his face yet." She strains to look, then grabs my arm. "Oh shit! Oh *shit!*"

"What?"

"It *him*! It's *Quelvin*!" She says, breathlessly, then laughs. "Not funny."

"He's big," she says. "But not huge. What's the word I'm searching for?"

"Sturdy? Solid? Chiseled? Impossibly handsome?"

"Impossibly handsome is two words. He actually looks super-familiar. Like..."

"That actor guy, right?"

"Exactly! Uh...What's he doing?"

"I never know."

"You're *positive* he's on our side?"

"We're still alive, aren't we?"

"Don't let him separate us, okay?"

"Okay. Same goes for you, okay?"

We laugh nervously. Presley says, "How long till we'll feel safe?"

"The answer to that is a mixture between never and always. But if he hugs me, it's a good sign."

When we climb out, he *does* happen to hug me, and Presley shows me a "thumbs-up."

Now the three of us are in a military-style Hummer, like the kind you used to see in civilian car dealerships years ago before gas prices doubled.

Presley says, "Where are you taking us, Mr. Creed?"

He says, "To a nondescript, but charming, hunter's cabin that's located—" He glances at me in the rear-view mirror before adding: "—in the middle of...nowhere." This, so I'd know his helicopter is wired for sound, and he heard all our conversations, including how handsome he is, which is good, but he also heard me say you can't feel completely safe around him, and also how if he hugged me it was a good sign.

Does that mean he hugged me to give us a false sense of security? And if so, does that mean his motives toward us are sinister?

I blurt out: "Presley wants you to promise you won't kidnap, kill, or torture us."

"*I never said that!*" Presley snaps, indignantly. Then adds, "But I *should* have."

"Sorry," Creed says.

Presley and I exchange a look, then instinctively glance at the door locks to see if we can bail if we have to. But Creed follows up on his comment by saying, "I didn't mean to frighten you. I'm taking you to the safest place imaginable."

"What about Sophie?" I ask.

"What about her?"

"She's not happy we left her behind."

He says, "I only needed Press, but considering all she's been through I didn't think she'd feel safe coming alone."

"*Press?*" I say with enough annoyance to cause him to glance at me again.

Presley says, "You're right. I wouldn't have come without Dani. No way."

Creed glances at me again, only this time his eyes are smiling. Mine smile back as if we're secretly saying, *Presley thinks she had a choice in the matter.*

"You're not making us wear blindfolds or hoods?" I ask.

Presley glares at me.

I shrug. "He usually blindfolds me."

"Not necessary," Creed says.

Okay, so that means he really *is* taking us somewhere safe, or it doesn't matter where we're going because we're never going to leave.

After ten minutes of driving, he stops the vehicle and hands us hoods. Presley whines, "I thought you said—"

Creed interrupts her: "We're about to leave the first set of woods. *Now* the hoods are necessary."

We put them on and immediately lose track of time, so I'll just say we drive another 30 minutes, more or less, on what feels like a highway, before feeling the Hummer pull off the road. Then we travel several miles at a very slow pace over an extremely bumpy surface, then slow down and descend into what we learn—after removing our hoods—is a giant underground parking garage.

While I have no idea where we are, or what this place is, I know an underground bunker when I see one. I look at Presley and say: "He's captured Quelvin."

Presley looks at Creed. "Is that true?"

"It is," he says. "Are you up for a visit?"

"No."

"Very well. You can watch through the one-way glass."

I say, "How could you possibly catch him this quickly?"

"I called in the favor."

My eyes must have bugged out, because he laughed at my expression before saying, "I knew you'd tell Presley. That was okay with me, since I purposely misled you about the guy who owed the favor."

"Misled me how?"

Creed says, "He wouldn't answer any of my questions unless I called in the favor. So I did, because I'm a Level 1 friend to you, and he told me everything I told you, plus Quelvin's name and address. One of my guys had Quelvin in the back of a paneled truck within hours after I called you back."

"What made you think I'd tell Presley?"

"Please."

I frown. "I mean, at what point did you know for *certain* I was going to tell her?"

He laughs. "The moment I said, 'Don't tell Presley!'"

The frown remains on my face, but deepens. "Am I really so predictable?"

"You are. To me, anyway. But that's not a bad thing."

He hands me a folded piece of paper. I open it and instantly feel the red creeping into my neck and face.

Presley notices it and says, "What does it say?"

I hand her the note.

She laughs.

Creed laughs.

The note says: *Am I really so predictable?*

I glare at him. "I might surprise you one day!"

He hands me another folded piece of paper that I refuse to open. Instead, I tear it into pieces and throw them on the floor.

He reaches into his pocket and holds up another note that's been torn into pieces and taped back together. That note says, *I might surprise you one day!*

He grins like an idiot, and Presley howls with laughter.

"Fuck you both!" I say.

"You know I love you, Dani," Creed says.

I show him my best fake smile. "I know you do, Donovan. Are you going to personally drive us back to the helicopter when we're finished here?"

"Yes. Why?"

"Your pilot's got our handbags, but inside mine is a bag of the best jellybeans I've ever tasted. You really need to try them."

"I would," he says, "but I'm trying to get a little less beetle shit in my diet."

I try to punch his arm, but he catches my fist in his giant hand, smiles, and says, "You seem upset. Maybe I shouldn't give you the last note."

"*Applesauce!*"

"Excuse me?"

"If your note says applesauce, I'll drop to my knees and blow you right here in the parking garage. If it doesn't, you'll have to admit I'm not predictable."

He laughs like I've never seen him laugh before. Then hands me the final note.

I hold my breath as I open it, half expecting to see the word applesauce on it, but it doesn't say that at all.

What it *does* say is: *Okay, I admit you're not predictable.*

I frown, and show the note to Presley, who—bless her heart—doesn't laugh. She shows me the cutest expression to show me she thinks Creed's teasing has gone too far, and gives me the sweetest hug, and I feel something stir inside me, and remember this is how it started with the school teacher, so I mentally remove the batteries from *that* toy to keep it from getting turned on by accident.

"Sorry Dani," Creed says. "But you deserved it for breaking your promise. Let's go pay Quelvin a visit."

As he leads us toward the lone steel door, I say, "I never actually *promised* not to tell Presley. And if you pull a piece of paper from your pocket that *says* that, I'll stick it up your ass!"

Chapter 36

CREED HOLDS THE DOOR OPEN FOR US, THEN leads us to an elevator.

"How big is this place?" I ask.

"Two stories," he says. "Both below ground."

"All this for one guy?" Presley says.

Creed laughs. "It used to be a military facility. Now it's a hospital."

"With a cabin on top?"

"That's right. If you happened upon it all you'd see is the cabin above us, which is filled with hidden state-of-the-art surveillance equipment."

"What happens if someone tries to break into it, or use it for a hunting cabin, or romantic weekend getaway?"

"You've heard of unmarked graves?"

Presley nods.

He winks. "We've got unmarked cemeteries!"

He presses the elevator button and says, "I acquired the property a couple years ago, renovated it, and turned it into a private hospital. Quelvin's in the basement, in an interrogation room."

The elevator doors open, we get in.

"You left Quelvin there *alone?*" I say.

"He's with Callie."

I check Presley's face and hair.

"Fuck."

"What's wrong?" she says.

She's flawless. That's what's wrong.

"Nothing," I say. Presley's getting ready to see Quelvin, the man who's brutalized her body and terrorized her mind for years. No sense in dragging her into my little hell of insecurity. I want to ask her how I look. Creed realizes this, and rolls his eyes.

"I saw that!" I say.

"Are you afraid?" Presley says.

"No. Just anxious."

Creed looks like he's about to say something, but I glare him into rethinking it. We're about to see the Callie Carpenter, the prettiest woman on the planet, and he knew this when he called me at Sophie's at 2 a.m. and *still* only gave us ten lousy minutes to get ready. And while Presley used them to get all dolled up, I wasted them arguing with Sofe. Creed's pilot still has our handbags, which means, no mirrors, no hairbrush, no makeup, and....

The elevator stops.

The doors open.

We walk into a small lobby that has a steel door on each of three walls. Creed leads us to the one on the right, peers into the retinal scanner, waits for the click, then leads us into a room like you see on TV, where detectives interrogate witnesses. Except that this room has a large table, with four comfortable chairs, and a console in the center.

"Oh my God!" Presley says, putting her hand to her face.

I start to say, "I know. She's breathtaking!" But stop myself, realizing she's talking about Quelvin, who's standing naked, facing us, with wrists and ankles shackled to eye-bolts in the concrete wall. His lips are moving, but we hear no sounds.

Presley doesn't have to tell me "It's him!" but she does, anyway. Of course, she's told me the same thing about half the men we've encountered since the day I met her. But this really *is* him, and she finally knows it.

Without taking her eyes off Quelvin she says, "Why is he naked?"

"That was Callie's idea. She thought it would put you more at ease to see him at his most vulnerable, and help you realize, for the first time in your life, *you* have complete control over *him*."

"That's really thoughtful of her," Presley says, "but he's probably really embarrassed."

"Tough shit!" I say.

"Does his nudity make you uncomfortable?" Creed says. "We can cover his groin, if you like."

"I'm okay. It's just…I thought you were gonna *kill* him."

"That was the original plan," Creed says, "but this way's better."

"Why?"

"This way you won't have any doubts. If you have any unanswered questions, you can ask him now, and he'll answer honestly. Then we can punish and kill him however you wish, or *you* can do the punishing, or killing, if you wish. But after today, you'll never have to wonder if he's after you, because you'll be here when we pronounce him dead."

"If I ask him a question," she says, "How will I know he's telling the truth?"

"He's been our guest for several days, and knows not to lie. About anything." He glances at my face and says, "Why the skeptical look, Dani?"

"How can Presley trust him to tell the truth?" I say. "Yes, I get that he's *been* here several days. But you're implying he's been tortured, and that's clearly not the case."

"What are you basing *that* on?" Creed says.

"He's completely unmarked!"

"So it appears. Then again, you're only seeing his front side."

"How bad have you hurt him?" Presley says.

Creed flips a switch, and we hear Quelvin moaning, crying, begging Callie not to hurt him anymore.

And now I see the small pool of blood behind his ankles. There's a drain there, but the blood is pooling slightly faster than the drain can handle.

Presley says, "Can I see his other side?"

Creed says, "Yes, but trust me: you don't want to."

She turns to me. "Dani?"

I say, "In my experience, when a guy says 'trust me, you don't want to see' something, he's usually right."

She nods.

Creed offers us seats at his console. "Press? Is there something you'd like to ask him?"

"How do I do it?"

"See the little toggle switch in front of you on the console? Push it forward when you want to speak, and pull it back if you want to say something you don't want him to hear."

She presses the switch forward and says:

Chapter 37

"MR. QUELVIN? I'M PRESLEY AYERS. DO YOU REMEMBER ME?"

Quelvin looks up toward our window. Creed whispers, "Don't worry. He can't see you."

"I'm not worried," she says.

To Quelvin, Callie says, "She asked you a question, Tony."

Presley flips the toggle. "Why's she calling him Tony?"

"His birth name was Tony DiPalma."

"I knew it!" I say.

Creed looks at me. "You knew his name was Tony DiPalma?"

"Not exactly. But I knew it couldn't be Adam Elliott."

"Elliott's the first name he used in WITSEC," Creed says.

"I know," I say, smugly.

He rolls his eyes again.

Presley flips the toggle forward and says, "Mr. Quelvin? I asked if you remembered me."

Callie takes a single step toward him and he quickly says, "Yes! Yes, I remember! I'm so sorry...for...everything. Please forgive me! I—"

Callie growls, "No speeches, Tony. Just answer the questions."

He looks pleadingly up at the window, but says nothing.

Presley says, "Mr. Quelvin?"

"Y-yes?"

"Do you know that I can see your pee pee?"

Chapter 38

PRESLEY ASKED HIM LOTS OF QUESTIONS, INCLUDING:

"Was I the first?" (Yes)

"What made you choose me?" (You were the prettiest. And the nicest. And I hated your mother!)

"What were you thinking about the first time you raped me?" (My birthday.)

"Say out loud what you were thinking when you were hurting me, and I was crying my eyes out." (I can have anything I want because it's my birthday.)

"Did you feel badly afterward?" (No.)

"What were you thinking about the second time you raped me? (How good it felt.)

"How many girls have you raped?" (Ten.)

"How many women?" (Just you, so far.)

"What do you know about the mob that they don't want you to tell in court?"

"Don't answer that!" Callie said. Then Creed told Presley she couldn't ask any questions about the mob.

"Why not?" she asked.

"It would put your life, and Dani's, in danger."

"How would anyone find out?"

"I don't know. Maybe you'll be under hypnosis someday, or in a hospital bed, sedated, recovering from an operation. It's just safer if you honestly don't know."

"Can I ask if he's ever killed anyone?"

"No."

—What Creed *isn't* saying makes a light bulb go off in my head: of *course* Sophie wasn't allowed to come with us! Her Uncle Sal's the mob boss of the entire Midwest! Quelvin has probably been waiting all these years to testify against Uncle Sal!

She also asked some questions to make sure he's the right guy, like, "What was your room number at our school?" (Room 4) and, "Who was your favorite poet?" (Emerson) and, "What was your dog's name?" (I can't remember.)

When Quelvin said that, Creed frowned and said, "We can *make* him remember."

But Presley said, "No, he got it right. That was the dog's actual name: I Can't Remember."

When all her questions were asked and answered, Creed said, "Press, would you like to punish him somehow?"

"No thank you."

"Would you like *us* to punish him?"

"No," she says. And then she says something that absolutely floors me:

Chapter 39

"I DON'T WANT HIM TO DIE," Presley says.

"Excuse me?"

"Not yet."

"Why not?"

"He needs to testify against those bad people. Otherwise, all this—the rapes he got away with—will have been for nothing."

Creed looks visibly frustrated, and I know why: those *bad* people he'd be testifying against are Creed's business associates. He *can't* let Quelvin go. He looks to me for help.

I say, "You have no idea what Donovan went through to get this man."

"I know," Presley says. "You told me about the gigantic favor he got from the Bavarian guy that owns his own village. Of course, I realize that was a metaphor."

"A metaphor for what?"

"The US Marshall who owed him a major favor."

I look at Creed.

He shrugs.

"Asshole!" I say.

Presley gives me an odd look, so I say, "Well, of course it was a metaphor. Those of us in the business never come right out and say things directly, in case our phones have been tapped."

She nods.

I say, "But the problem with letting Quelvin live, this trial could be delayed for months—"

"Years!" Creed says, picking up on my argument thread. He adds, "If we turn DiPalma—I mean, Quelvin—back over to the Marshalls, they'll simply change his name, relocate him, and he'll continue assaulting women, year after year."

"Not to mention you'll never have peace," I say. "You'll never be able to lead a normal life. You'll always worry he might be coming for you."

"And there's one last thing to consider," Creed says. "The US Marshall who owed me the favor? If we let Quelvin walk, he'll rat the Marshall out, and my friend will not only lose his job, but the mob will think he knows something, and will probably torture his family to find Quelvin."

"Okay," Presley says. "You can kill him. But I want to watch, so I'll know he's really dead."

"I think that's wise," Creed says.

"But I don't want him to suffer," she says.

"Callie can kill him in the space of four seconds."

"How?"

"She'll snap his neck. Or I can, if you prefer."

"If it's all the same to you, I'd like her to do it. It's only fitting he be killed by a woman. But you can be the one to cut his nuts out, if you like."

"*Excuse* me?" I say, recoiling in horror.

"I want both his balls," Presley says, matter-of-factly. "One for each time he raped me."

"What on earth would you *do* with them?"

"Dip them in gold and make a keychain out of them."

Creed says, "I *like* this girl!"

I frown. "Of course you do. Like her mom says, she's gorgeous."

"Is she?"

"Second prettiest woman in the world, I'm told."

"I hadn't noticed."

"I'll just bet you haven't!"

Epilogue

1. I'm disappointed in Presley for wanting to keep a souvenir.

Does it say something about her character that she dipped Quelvin's nuts in gold and keeps them on a key chain?
Probably not, but it bothers me for reasons that, like her keychain, I can't quite wrap my fingers around.
But Presley's famous now, and a multi-millionaire, and she did actually pay us our full rate, so I shouldn't complain. That said, I'd prefer her endorsement to her cash, since that would send my business through the roof, as in:

Dani Ripper: Private Detective to the Stars!

2. Unfortunately, we can't tell anyone we succeeded in finding her rapist, because if the US Marshalls find out, they'll put us in prison.

The mob knows. Don't know how *they* found out, but the dozen boxes I've received, filled with thousands of dollars of untraceable bills, makes it pretty clear they're happy about it. Maybe I'll be:

Dani Ripper: Private Detective to the Mob!

This is so typical. Seems like every time I solve a case, I can't advertise it. So once again I'll have to smile and keep my mouth shut.

It's like when one of your girlfriends asks you to fly with her to Wisconsin to spend the weekend at her lake house, and tells you how great her dad is, and you meet him, expecting great things, but catch him constantly checking out your ass. Sunday morning, you see him coming out of the guest room where you packed your suitcase, and when you get home you're missing a bra and panties. You can't tell your girlfriend what happened, but at her next party, when she tells everyone what a prince her dad is, you feel like the world's biggest douche for not chiming in.

3. I took Presley's advice and gave the Butter Man a pat of butter.

He stared at it in disbelief, then fell to his knees and sang all four verses of Leonard Cohen's *Hallelujah* at the top of his lungs. Next time I saw him he was *inside* my office, dressed impeccably, informing me I was about to get a rent increase! Turns out the reason he used to stand in front of the building is because he owns it, and when the butter thing drove him crazy, his kids took over for him, and didn't really pay much attention to details like automatic rent increases and such. There's a lesson here, ladies: give a man exactly what he wants, and it'll cost you, every time.

4. Fanny scammed us again!

Her whole deal about the community of polygraph operators was total BS. I mean, sure, there aren't many of them, but imagine our surprise when we learned—quite by accident—that Archie the polygraph guy had been living with Fanny more than a month before administering Chelsea's test. That means Fanny's "taking one for the team" was a huge overstatement, and a great job of acting on her part. Dillon and I would love to either nominate her for an Oscar, or get our $500 back, but since our business requires getting polygraph tests on short notice, we're going to pretend we don't know about her and Archie's relationship.

It does bother me to think that Archie might be teaching Fanny how to beat the machine, given her history of filing lawsuits against former employers...

5. I finally found out how the real James Quelvin lost his nose!!!

As you know, this issue has driven me crazy since the day I met him, but now, thanks to Sophie, I finally got my answer. And, of course, it makes perfect sense, once you hear the story.

But you've been kind enough to bear with me through this entire adventure, and I don't want to impose on your good will any longer than necessary. Plus, you might accuse the author of padding his word count. So unless you're like me, and just *have* to know how Quelvin lost his nose, I'll end the story right here:

THE END

PS: If you *are* like me, and just *have* to know, access the following link, and I'll give you the scoop:

https://daniripper.wordpress.com/books/dont-tell-presley/

Author's Note

AN ESTIMATED 71% OF ALL RAPISTS ARE SERIAL OFFENDERS. While it's not a pleasant experience to endure a rape kit procedure, the girls and women who go through the process are heroes, far as I'm concerned. As such, they deserve to have their kits tested. But are they being tested?

In many cases, the answer is no.

In 2004 the Justice Department revealed 221,000 rape kits had not been tested. Thankfully, Congress passed the Debbie Smith Act, which provided hundreds of millions of dollars to fund the processing of DNA evidence from untested rape kits. As a result, thousands of suspects have been identified.

But more work needs to be done. Tens of thousands of kits across the country are still sitting in storage, unexamined. And every day these kits sit on shelves, the rapists get another 24 hours to hunt new victims.

The forensic evidence is going untested for two reasons: the cost; and/or because prosecutors consider the cases unwinnable in court. Both excuses are unacceptable. Rape kit processing generally costs approximately $1,500 per kit. As for being unwinnable, every DNA match could get a serial rapist off the street. If, as a prosecutor, you knew the next kit on the shelf would prevent your daughter or sister from being attacked, you'd find a way to get it tested.

The girls and women waiting for rape kit evidence to be processed have been through hell, and deserve justice. But just as important, the processing of these kits could prevent untold thousands of future rapes. I hope you will join me in helping to spread awareness about this crucial issue.

Personal Message from John Locke:

I love writing books! But what I love even more is hearing from readers. If you enjoyed this or any of my other books it would mean the world to me if you'd click the link below so you can be on my notification list. That way you can receive updates, contests, prizes, and savings of up to 67% on eBooks immediately after publication!

Just access this link: http://www.DonovanCreed.com, and I'll personally thank you for trying my books.

Also, if you get a chance, I hope you'll check out Dani's website:

http://www.DaniRipper.wordpress.com

John Locke

New York Times Best Selling Author

8th Member of the Kindle Million Sales Club

(Members include James Patterson, George R.R. Martin, and Lee Child)

John Locke had 4 of the top 10 eBooks on Amazon/Kindle at the same time, including #1 and #2!

...Had 6 of the top 20 books <u>at the same time</u>!

...Had 8 books in the top 43 <u>at the same time</u>!

...Has written 27 books in five years in <u>six separate genres</u>, <u>All best-sellers</u>!

...Has been published throughout the world in numerous languages by the world's most prestigious publishing houses!

...Winner, Second Act Magazine's Story of the Year!

...Named by Time Magazine as one of the "Stars of the DIY-Publishing Era"

Wall Street Journal: "John Locke (is) transforming the 'book' business"

JOHN LOCKE

New York Times Best Selling Author
#1 Best Selling Author on Amazon Kindle

Donovan Creed Series:
Lethal People
Lethal Experiment
Saving Rachel
Now & Then
Wish List
A Girl Like You
Vegas Moon
The Love You Crave
Maybe
Callie's Last Dance
Because We Can!
This Means War!

Emmett Love Series:
Follow the Stone
Don't Poke the Bear!
Emmett & Gentry
Goodbye, Enorma
Rag Soup

Dani Ripper Series:
Call Me!
Promise You Won't Tell?
Teacher, Teacher
Don't Tell Presley!

Dr. Gideon Box Series:
Bad Doctor
Box
Outside the Box

Other:
Kill Jill
Casting Call

Young Adult:
A Kiss for Luck (Kindle Only)

Non-Fiction:
How I Sold 1 Million eBooks in 5 Months!

Made in the USA
Middletown, DE
21 July 2015